'ou're a fraud, Liam O'Sullivan!"

ooked at her as she spoke. "Tough guy. Calm, cool
collected. Ice in your veins. All the things people
about you? None of it's true."

ıre, it is."

esterday I thought you were in control and ready to
d out we're having a baby. But today you're more
rvous than I am. Let's face it. Your family's going to
as shocked about this as mine. And equally
ısapproving."

le reached out for her. "I d   I only
:are about you and th

But we can't d   ing
ito this relations   ing
ur history."

Ve don't have a hi   s our parents' history.
e were both raised   natred for each other's family.
ıt this child will end that cycle. Or his grandparents
on't be part of his life."

ou know me. That can never happen."

shot her that smoky look that got her in this
edicament in the first place. The one she could never
ist.

h, I know you," he said in a throaty voice. "I know
ery inch of you…intimately. And I can't wait to know
u again."

Rid

MARRIED TO
THE MUM-TO-BE

BY
HELEN LACEY

First Published in Great Britain 2017
By Mills & Boon, an imprint of HarperCollins*Publishers*
1 London Bridge Street, London, SE1 9GF

© 2017 Helen Lacey

ISBN: 978-0-263-92292-9

23-0417

Our policy is to use papers that are natural, renewable and recyclable products and made from wood grown in sustainable forests. The logging and manufacturing processes conform to the legal environmental regulations of the country of origin.

Printed and bound in Spain
by CPI, Barcelona

Helen Lacey grew up reading *Black Beauty* and *Little House on the Prairie*. These childhood classics inspired her to write her first book when she was seven, a story about a girl and her horse. She loves writing for Mills & Boon Cherish, where she can create strong heroes with a soft heart and heroines with gumption who get their happily-ever-after. For more about Helen, visit her website, www.helenlacey.com.

For Robert
To the moon and back... always.

Chapter One

"I think I'm pregnant."

Kayla Rickard hadn't planned on announcing the news to Liam O'Sullivan that way.

But the unexpected craving for pistachio ice cream at nine that Tuesday morning, followed by a surge of nausea that had her racing to the bathroom to lose the contents of her stomach, and *then* staring at her pale reflection in the washroom mirror, had her realizing one undeniable and alarming fact.

I'm pregnant.

She didn't really need an over-the-counter test or a doctor to tell her what was now seeping through to her bones with Technicolor clarity, even though she would certainly get confirmation as soon as she could. Because it all made perfect sense. She was late. And she was *never* late. She was nauseous, notably in the mornings. And she'd been uncharacteristically weary for weeks. Her breasts were tender. Her senses were heightened. And now these random cravings? The more she'd considered it, the more obvious it became.

"What?"

Liam's hollow voice broke through her thoughts. Kayla took a deep breath, squared her shoulders and looked him over…every perfectly proportioned inch of his six-foot-two frame. His short, dark brown hair was cut neatly and his features were flawlessly put together. He was *turn-your-head* handsome. And successful and confident and sexy as sin. His midnight-blue gaze met hers and Kayla was drawn deep into him. It was always like that between them. There was tension and heat and raw, undeniable attraction…

And now, God help them, there would be a baby, too.

"I'm…you know. *Late*," she whispered, the words curdling deep in her throat.

The moment he realized what she meant his expression turned to a kind of wary bewilderment. He stared at her, searching her face with his eyes. "Are you sure?"

"No," she replied quickly, dropping her voice again. "I mean, I'm sure that I'm late, but I'm not sure about anything else. But I…I feel like I am. Which probably doesn't make any sense because I wouldn't be too far along. But I feel…I don't know…*different*."

He was silent, looking at her with hot, blistering intensity. There were questions in his eyes and tension in his jaw. "We obviously need to talk about this."

"Not here," she said, looking around the reception area. "People might see us and—"

"My office?" he suggested quietly.

Kayla nodded. She'd been to his office many times, mostly to discuss the upcoming charity benefit for the local hospital that was being held at the museum and art gallery where she was the curator. And the extension plans for the gallery that were currently being reviewed by the local council.

He looked tense and guilt snapped at her heels. It had come out all wrong. She'd planned on going somewhere private and quietly letting him know she suspected she was pregnant...not announcing the fact in the middle of the hotel foyer with his staff and guests watching on.

The O'Sullivans were the wealthiest and most powerful family in Cedar River, a small town that sat in the shadow of the Black Hills of South Dakota. And Liam was the heir apparent to the O'Sullivan portfolio and fortune. Both his brothers lived elsewhere—Kieran was a doctor in Sioux Falls and Sean was a movie producer in LA. Liam had returned to Cedar River after college and taken over from his father when he retired, running the big hotel in town, along with several other businesses.

Kayla followed him wordlessly toward the elevator and by the time they reached his second-floor office she was a bundle of nerves. She looked around as she crossed the threshold. "Where's Connie?" she asked.

"Lunch," he replied and checked his watch. "So we have about fifteen minutes until she gets back to her desk."

Connie had been Liam's assistant for several years and Kayla liked the other woman a lot—but she didn't want anyone's prying eyes around them while they discussed her bombshell.

She walked farther into the room and then followed him into his large office. "Okay."

"You do look a little pale," he said as he closed the door. "You were sick last week," he said, almost as though he was talking to himself. "I should have realized."

Kayla shrugged and said lightly, "Well, it only occurred to me after I threw up today, so don't beat yourself up."

"Will pregnancy complicate your condition?"

Kayla had suffered from anemia since she was a teen-ager. A heavy menstrual cycle and her vegetarian lifestyle meant she had to keep the condition under control with her diet and exercise. She would certainly be asking her doctor about any precautions or supplements she'd need to take if she was pregnant.

"I'm sure it will be fine. And I didn't mean to tell you in the middle of the lobby," she admitted. "It just slipped out that way."

"It's okay," Liam said as he moved to the small kitch-enette in the corner of the office and grabbed a bottle of water from the bar fridge. "I'm always glad to see you."

More guilt pressed between her shoulder blades. It had been three days since they'd been this close. Her doing, not his. She was the one putting distance between them, stepping back and finding excuses to stay away. But there was no stepping back from this. A baby would change ev-erything.

Kayla instinctively pressed a hand to her belly. Even without a test, she knew she had a baby growing inside her... *Liam's baby*. Every instinct she possessed told her it was true.

"Why don't you sit down," he said and passed the bot-tle to her.

Kayla took the water and stared at him. "You seem aw-fully calm."

"Hysterics won't help."

She gave a brittle laugh and he immediately gave her an inquiring look. "I'm trying to imagine you being hys-terical."

He ignored her words and pointed to the dark leather sofa pushed against one wall. "Come and sit down, Kayla."

She walked across the room and sat down. He was a few

strides behind her and then perched on the armrest, elbows on his knees. "You said you were late. How late?"

She held up one hand. "Five or six days. But last month I had an unusually light period," she said candidly, figuring there was little point in being coy about the whole thing. "And you know I'm paranoid about keeping track of my cycle to avoid any bouts of anemia."

He was silent for a moment, clearly absorbing her words. "I take it you haven't been to see a doctor or done a home test?"

"Not yet. I didn't want to go to Talbot's Drugstore. If I buy a pregnancy test in this town, word would spread like wildfire."

"I can go and get it."

"No," she said, her tone growing frantic. "That would be worse."

It sounded overly dramatic, but it was the truth. And Liam didn't disagree. Cedar River was a small town, and small towns weren't easy to get lost in. He nodded fractionally, as though he was working out a solution. And of course he came up with one. In typical Liam fashion.

"We could drive into Rapid City this afternoon and buy whatever test is needed."

"Not today," she said and shook her head. "Tomorrow," she added, thinking that Rapid City, a forty-minute drive from Cedar River, was far enough away that she wouldn't be recognized. "I still feel a little queasy. And anyway, I can go by myself, so there's no need to—"

"Kayla," he said softly, cutting her off. "We should go together."

Of course he was right. And she didn't want to exclude him. But she also didn't want him thinking he could snap his fingers and she'd simply comply.

"I didn't tell you so you could make all the decisions, Liam. Stop being so bossy."

"Habit," he said and his mouth twitched as he sat back. "You know how I am."

Yes, she knew. Better than anyone.

She got to her feet and walked toward the long window. The drapes were open and the street below was its usual bustle for a midweek lunchtime.

She loved Cedar River. After college in Washington State she'd returned home for two months, helping her father out at his real estate office. She knew there was nowhere in town she could utilize her degree and eventually got an opportunity to work at an art museum in Colorado. It meant leaving again, but she had to do what was best for her career. The next few years she'd spent working in Denver had been good ones, but something had always been missing from her life. She'd enjoyed her work, made friends, dated and eventually had a three-year relationship with a college professor during her time there. But there had been a hollowness to her life. An emptiness. A space that she couldn't fill with work or friends or a romantic relationship. A space she needed to fill with one thing.

Home.

Cedar River had called her back. When the long-serving museum curator retired and the position became available, she had immediately applied, and with her stellar references had quickly been offered the job. That was over a year ago. She'd had dreams back then…dreams of living back in town, of spending time with her friends and family, and then of meeting someone special, settling down and having a family of her own. Someone that *wasn't* Liam O'Sullivan.

Because her father absolutely hated his father…hated the entire O'Sullivan family, in fact. And she knew it would break her parents' heart when they discovered she was in a relationship with the son of their mortal enemy.

She knew Liam, of course. Every girl in town knew the three handsome O'Sullivan brothers. And she'd always liked his younger sister, Liz. Since he was seven years older than Kayla, they had traveled in different social circles, but she remembered his youngest brother, Sean, from high school, even though he'd been a couple of grades above her. It seemed there were always girls hanging around the O'Sullivan boys. By the time she'd returned to town permanently, both Sean and Kieran had moved away. Liz had died tragically, leaving three young daughters and a husband behind, and Liam was running the hotel.

And she didn't give him a thought. Not one. Not ever. Until the night her car collided with his in the hotel parking area. She was backing out, he was driving in. His hulking black Silverado had barely sustained a scratch, but her aging Beamer wasn't as lucky. One broken taillight and a crumpled trunk later, she'd gotten out of the car full of apologies and then had clamped her mouth shut when she realized who she'd crashed into.

Because she'd been raised on a steady diet of dislike and abhorrence for anyone named O'Sullivan all of her life. The feud went back thirty years, before she was born. It was not a story that anyone talked about in detail. Her father and J.D. O'Sullivan had been friends once, even partners in business. But something had happened that had changed everything, and Kayla had always happily kept her distance, leaving for college and not giving the O'Sullivans a single thought. When she returned to visit her parents over the years, she would occasionally see Liam or even his brothers around town if they were visiting their family, but never entertained the idea of talking to any them. She went to the O'Sullivan pub with her friends and rarely registered Liam's presence. Of course, that changed once she returned home permanently and then crashed into Liam's truck a month later.

Immediately on the defensive, she'd expected him to be arrogant and judgmental and entitled about the whole incident. That's who he was—or at least, that's who she believed he was. And she did her best to ignore his handsome face, broad shoulders and how good he looked in jeans, white shirt and a leather jacket that screamed money and good taste. He was hot, no doubt about it. But he was also as off-limits as the stars from a distant planet.

He'd looked her up and down, quickly registering who she was and probably imagining the great big red flag waving between them just as she did. She saw a flicker of something in his eyes, a kind of unexpected and guarded awareness that was mirrored in her own.

But to her surprise, Liam had been very civil about the whole thing. They'd exchanged cell numbers and insurance details and he even called a tow for her and a cab once she'd refused his offer to drive her home. She said goodbye before one last apology and left. And that, she'd thought, was that.

Except he called her forty-eight hours later and asked her out.

Date Liam O'Sullivan?

Not a chance.

She refused him as politely as she could and pushed the idea from her thoughts. Until three days later when he called again. Of course she turned him down. There was no way in hell she could go out with him. Even if she wanted to. Which of course she didn't. At least, not without hurting her parents.

Instead, she started dating someone else. Will Serrato was the foreman on one of the local ranches, a good-looking cowboy with nice manners, a lovely smile and no familial ties to Cedar River, which suited her fine. Her parents liked him and Kayla enjoyed his company. It lasted three months, until they both admitted they were better off as friends rather than lovers. She liked Will a lot, but that wasn't enough to sustain a long-term relationship. She'd had three bland years with the college professor as proof. *Liking* someone didn't cut it.

"Have you told anyone else?"

Liam's voice jerked her back into the moment. She turned and discovered he was only a couple of feet away. He had the stealth of a cat. Her blood heated immediately, her usual reaction when he was within touching distance.

She crossed her arms. "No."

"Not the Happy-Hour Crew?"

She frowned. That's what he called her friends, Ash, Lucy and Brooke. They'd regularly met at O'Sullivans on a Friday evening up until a few months ago. But Brooke had recently married a New York lawyer who'd bought out a legal practice in town and they'd adopted a baby girl who was biologically Brooke's niece. And Lucy and her fiancé Brant Parker were to marry in the next few months. Ash had a twelve-year-old son at home, plus a small ranch where she took in foster kids, and there wasn't much time left in the week for socializing.

"No one," she said again. "This is between me and you."

His mouth flattened. She knew that look. He was close, so close she could feel the heat radiating from him. Since they hadn't been as near to one another for days he was burning even hotter than usual. They had great chemistry and making love with him was like nothing she'd experienced before. Hot, passionate and yet achingly tender. For five months she'd loved him...*loved him*...with her body and her whole heart.

"I guess everyone will know soon enough," he said quietly, reaching down to briefly rest his hand against her belly.

Kayla stilled at his warm touch and felt cold when he moved his hand away. She didn't want to think about the whole world learning about her pregnancy. Confirming the news aloud to him—and to herself—was dramatic enough. "I have no intention of saying too much too soon, even if I do see my friends on a Thursday night."

"When you're hanging out at the Loose Moose?" he queried.

Kayla shrugged. Lucy's fiancé owned the Loose Moose, and although it was a different kind of place than O'Sullivans, it was still competition. And Liam knew she went there every other Thursday evening to have dinner with her friends. Brant was always there because he owned the place and Brooke regularly brought Tyler on their get-togethers. But Kayla had not taken Liam...not once. She didn't want the questions she would get from her friends. Or their concern, since they knew about the feud between her father and J.D. O'Sullivan.

"It's a nice place," she said extra sweetly. "The steaks are good."

His gaze narrowed. "You're a vegetarian."

Kayla managed a tight smile. "I like the salad bar," she said and shrugged lightly.

His hand came up to touch her cheek and as his fingertips gently rubbed her jawline the sensation spread heat through her with the speed of a brushfire. "I know what you like."

His words were packed with innuendo. He did know. Better than anyone. "Well, I guess I should get back to work."

"Not yet," he said, his voice so quiet it was almost a whisper. He leaned in closer, his intent obvious. She'd craved his kiss since that first date and tilted her chin acceptingly. He kissed the corner of her mouth softly. And then her cheek and then the sensitive spot just below her earlobe. "Come home with me tonight, Kayla," he whispered against her skin. "Come home and let me make love to you."

It should have been easy to nod and fall into his arms and to agree to anything he suggested. But it wasn't. If she *was* pregnant, then their complicated relationship was about to become even more so.

"I can't," she replied, woozy from the feel of his lips trailing over her skin. "Ash is coming by this evening to drop off some flyers for the hospital benefit. You know she's on one of the committees and is helping me with the—"

He pulled back, straightened and stared down at her. "Is this because of the fight we had the other day?"

She remembered the words they'd exchanged a few days earlier. It was the same discussion they'd been having since the beginning of their relationship. But she wasn't ready to break her father's heart. And she wouldn't be pushed.

"Was that a fight?" she asked and sighed.

He shrugged loosely. "Maybe. If it was, then I'm sorry."

Kayla reached out and touched his jaw, felt the bristle of stubble and smiled. "You didn't shave this morning?"

He met her gaze. "I don't sleep well unless I have you next to me. Then I woke up late and ran out of time."

His words melted her. She didn't want to give him sleepless nights. She didn't want to argue with him, either. She wanted…she wanted it to work out. She wanted their families to end the feuding. With a heavy heart, Kayla suspected she wanted the impossible.

"Liam…"

"It kills me to be away from you," he admitted and swallowed hard. His gaze dropped to her stomach and without a word he gently pressed a hand to her middle. "Do you really think that you're…" His words trailed off with a kind of agonized sigh when she nodded. "My god, Kayla…if you are then everything changes. Everything," he said again, steadier, as though he was affirming the idea to himself.

His palm was warm against her belly. And strong and familiar. Their connection had never seemed more intense than it did in that moment and she had to say what was on her mind. And in her heart. "This isn't what I planned… at least, not yet. But, the more I think about it, the more I want this baby, Liam. Despite what it will mean to our families. Despite how…complicated it is."

They hadn't talked about having children, not in any real depth. It was one of those things that seemed too hard, considering they were keeping their relationship a secret from everyone they knew. From the world.

"So do I, Kayla."

Of course she knew that. Liam would make a great father. "So, I'll see you tomorrow," she said and dropped her hand. "Okay?"

He nodded resignedly. "I'll pick you up in the morning at eight thirty and we'll drive into Rapid City."

Kayla frowned. "My mother is coming by in the morning, plus I have a busload of tourists arriving tomorrow, so it will have to wait until the afternoon before I—"

"You could cancel your mother and get Shirley to cover you," he said. "This really can't wait."

Sixtysomething Shirley had been working part-time at the museum for over twenty years and would certainly work if Kayla needed her. She pushed down her impatience at his high-handed logic. "Stop telling me what to do, Liam."

"I'm not trying to make things harder here, Kayla. But

if I'm going to be a father I'd like to know sooner rather than later."

Of course he would. Kayla had a fleeting thought that she was being selfish. She'd had all morning to get used to the idea. Liam had only had fifteen minutes. "Okay," she said agreeably. "Okay... I'll call Shirley when I get back to work. And my mother," she added.

His mouth twisted a little, as though he'd won a round. "I'll call you later."

She knew he would. He called her every night.

She grabbed her bag and headed for the door, stopping when he said her name. "What?"

"So I know that you're okay, text me when you get back to the apartment this afternoon."

The apartment. Not *her* apartment. Liam had his mind set on her spending every night at the house by the river. But she wasn't ready for that. Not yet. Not until her parents knew about their relationship. Sure, she was stalling. But she had her reasons and they were valid. Even if Liam did struggle to understand, Kayla knew she had to do what she thought was right. As she always had.

"I really am fine," she lied. "I mean, despite the fact that I'm probably pregnant and the baby is going to be caught in the middle of two families who hate one another."

His jaw tightened. "Kayla, you know that I will never allow that to happen. If you are pregnant, then our child will come first, before any old squabbles, before any decades-old resentment, before *anything*."

She shivered, because again she knew she should have been reassured. She knew Liam, she knew he could be ruthless when he needed to be. And she knew their relationship would be blown out of the water the moment her pregnancy was confirmed...and that Liam would be the one to do so.

"Of course I know that," she said quietly. "My month is nearly up, remember?"

Three and half weeks earlier they'd agreed she would tell her parents about their relationship. It wasn't an ultimatum. It was the next step. The obvious step. Exactly what needed to happen if they were to make their relationship work. But she still hadn't told them. Not because she was a coward, although sometimes she wondered if Liam thought that of her…but because her parents loved her so dearly and upsetting them was such an alien concept to her. Liam didn't appreciate that… Oh, he was considerate and caring, but he didn't truly understand her motives.

"I didn't suggest a month to hurt you," he said quietly. "Or push you. I just thought it would be long enough for you to broach the subject and maybe ease them into the idea."

"I know," she flipped back. "And I get that you don't understand the relationship I have with my parents. I get that you believe they smother me and think the world revolves around me…and you're right…they do. That still doesn't mean I want to upset them."

"I know you don't," he said. "I don't think anyone chooses to hurt the people they love."

Her throat thickened. It was a direct hit. He loved her. She loved him. It shouldn't be so messy. But it was.

"I'll talk to you later," she said and left the room before he had a chance to respond.

By the time she got back to the museum her head was throbbing. She turned the shingle over to say the place was open, unlocked the door and headed inside. As always, she experienced a sense of calm as she crossed the threshold. It always did that to her. The museum was her safe place. Her harbor. The balm she needed to soothe her soul. Split into two areas, it was a museum and art gallery, showcasing not only the incredible history of the town, but both the local and indigenous artists. There was a small gift shop that Shirley managed for a few hours each day, but mostly Kayla worked alone. And she liked it that way. Oh, she loved her family and friends, but the museum and gallery was her place, her calm center away from the world where she could think and read and find peace.

Liam understood that about her...perhaps more than anyone else ever had.

After she'd broken up with Will, Liam had pursued her again. Not obviously. In fact, at times he seemed to be ignoring her. But she knew what he was doing. The way he said her name whenever they met, the way his glittering blue eyes always seemed to linger on her mouth... Kayla was switched on enough to know she was being pursued. There was no ego in her realization, just instinct. An O'Sullivan had always been on the board of the museum, but suddenly he started turning up for the monthly meetings instead of his mother. And then he began regularly bringing his young nieces to the gallery. Subtle, for sure...but effective. Seeing him with the girls did something to her. It touched her heart, breaking down her defenses, making Kayla want him in ways that went beyond physical attraction.

It took a couple of months for Kayla to admit the truth to herself. That she liked him. That she *more* than liked him. And then one afternoon, when she could stand it no more, when he'd arrived early for a committee meeting to discuss the planned extension for the museum and they were alone in her office, she'd grabbed him by the lapel of his jacket and kissed him...forgetting everything...forgetting the three-decade-old feud, forgetting that her family would be devastated if they found out. All she knew was that in that moment, she had to feel his kiss, his touch.

It was also the moment she realized she was really falling for the son of the man her father hated most in the world.

So, from day one their relationship became a secret. No one could know. Her parents were good people, honest and hardworking, and they had always put her first. Always. And she wasn't eager to disrespect the love and devotion they had shown her all their lives.

Only...

If she was carrying Liam's child, hurting them was inevitable.

Her cell beeped with a text message as she walked into her office. She checked the number and saw that it was Ash saying she'd be at her apartment that afternoon. Kayla texted back, saying she'd see her later and then called her mother and rescheduled her visit. Then she called Shirley and asked her to cover her shift. Her cell rang again a few minutes later, and thinking it might be Shirley again and that something could be wrong, she snatched the phone up quickly.

"Hello," she said breathlessly.

"Hey, it's me. Liam." His deep voice wound through her system like silk.

Kayla managed to take a steadying breath. "What do you want?" She knew she sounded terse and unfriendly, but her patience was frayed.

"Just to see how you are."

"You saw me half an hour ago," she reminded him. "Not much has changed since then."

He was silent for a moment. "I *am* allowed to be concerned about you."

"I know that," she said, quickly hating how mean and short-tempered she must sound to him. "I'm sorry," she said and sighed. "I'm just tired. I'll feel better tomorrow."

He took a moment before he spoke again. "Thank you

for telling me. I know you could have kept this to yourself until you got confirmation."

"If I'm pregnant then it's your baby, too, Liam," she said softly, feeling a heady warmth spread through her limbs as the words left her mouth. "I'm not about to exclude you from anything. We're in this together."

"Are we?" he asked and her insides constricted.

"Yes," she replied. "We are."

He sighed heavily. "Kayla, you do know what this will mean, don't you?"

Tension filled her chest. "I don't want to think about it. Before I start thinking about what any of this means, I need to make sure. We *both* need to be sure."

"Of course," he said. "But if you are pregnant then we'll have to make some changes."

Oh, she knew. Reveal their relationship to the world. And hurt her parents in the process.

"I know that," she replied hotly. "You don't need to keep reminding me."

"I didn't call to upset you," he said quietly. "That's the last thing I want."

"I know that, too," she acknowledged and sighed. "But I'm not accustomed to hurting my parents. I don't like how the idea makes me feel. I don't like knowing that they are going to think that I've betrayed them." She sighed heavily. "And in a way, they'll be right. I knew how my dad felt about your father...about your family. I mean, I've known it practically all my life. I was raised on it. But it still didn't stop me from falling in love with you."

Silence stretched out between them, filled with thick, relentless tension. When he spoke again his voice was unusually raspy. "I haven't heard you admit that for a while."

"Admit what?" she queried, but knew exactly what he meant.

And he was right. She hadn't said it for weeks. Not even when she was in his arms, making love with him, and he'd whisper the words to her with heart-melting passion.

"I love you, too, Kayla," he said so softly that the sound of his voice hit her directly in the center of her chest. "But, you know, perhaps you're thinking about this the wrong way. You might be imagining the worst for no reason. This situation may do exactly the opposite. It could bring everyone together."

It was a nice idea. But a fantasy. Derek Rickard was not the forgiving type. And J.D. O'Sullivan was no better. There was way too much bad blood between the two families to imagine that there could be any kind of truce.

"I know my father. And yours," she added. "He won't be any more pleased about this than my folks."

"Frankly, I don't care about that," he said bluntly. "I care about you. And if you're pregnant, then I'll care about our child. And I'll protect you both...always."

Heat rushed behind her eyes. Whatever Liam's faults, he was undeniably loyal and fiercely protective of their relationship. It made her love him even more. And it also made the situation much harder.

"I know you will...and I know you don't agree with the way I've handled things."

"Handled things?"

She heard the query in his voice. "Okay," she admitted. "The way I *haven't* handled things with my parents. If I'm pregnant, we both know they're going to be hurt and stunned by the news."

"You think that's going to shock them?" He drew in a long breath. "Wait until they find out that we're married."

Chapter Two

An impromptu Vegas wedding wasn't something Liam had ever imagined for himself. Nonetheless, that was what he'd had just under a month earlier. Kayla had been at a conference in Nevada and he'd joined her there so they could spend the weekend together without worrying about being discovered. It had been a whim, fueled by three passionate and heady days of endless lovemaking and many bottles of champagne. They'd bought rings, found a chapel and a minister who looked way too much like Elvis to be taken seriously, and gotten hitched to the Blues Brothers' soundtrack. It had been the happiest day of his life.

But it was followed by weeks of pretending they meant nothing to each other when they were around their friends, work colleagues and respective families.

And it was slowly breaking him.

He loved her and he wanted her in his life every day. Not just a couple of times a week, splitting time between her apartment and his house, snatching weekends together when they could. She wanted to wait to let everyone know they were married, and although he understood her motives, he didn't agree with them. He knew she didn't want to hurt her parents. But she was hurting their relationship with her silence. So when they'd come back from Vegas he'd pushed her a little, and finally got her to agree that they would both tell their parents by the end of the month. That was three and half weeks ago and they were no closer to a resolution.

And he had no idea if there ever would be.

All his life he'd been used to getting his own way…but not with Kayla. He stretched out his shoulders, so wound up he could barely stand being in his own skin. Only Kayla could make him feel that way. Only Kayla and her deep caramel eyes and perfectly proportioned features. She was easily the most beautiful woman he had ever known. But it wasn't just her looks that drew him in—everything about her affected him on a primal level. The night she'd crashed into his car everything had changed.

Gone was the lanky teenager he vaguely remembered was prom queen. Oh, she'd always been attractive, but maturity had given her poise and amplified her beauty.

Desire, raw and uncomplicated, as wild as a river, as untamed as the Black Hills, had coursed through every cell he possessed. So much so that Liam could barely recall what he'd said to her that night. All he could remember was Kayla, standing in the parking lot in her white dress and fringed, come-take-me cowgirl boots.

He wanted her. Despite his better judgment. Despite knowing that the long-running feud between their respective fathers would make it difficult.

Then he tried for two days to get her out of his system. And failed. He went on a date with another woman, thinking all he needed to do was get laid and that would end the constant images of Kayla bombarding his thoughts. But by eight o'clock he'd had enough and bailed, not feeling particularly proud of himself, but not prepared to sleep with one woman when he was thinking about another.

So, despite knowing it would be like walking a minefield, he'd called her up and asked her out. And got shot down like a duck in hunting season. He tried again three days later and when her answer was the same, decided he would forget all about her. When she started dating the cowboy he knew it was ridiculous to spend his nights thinking about her and for months he embarked on a series of meaningless one-night stands, but they did nothing to get his attraction for Kayla out of his system. Then she broke up with the cowboy and he had a clear playing field.

Still, she resisted him for months. And not having her, he discovered, made him want her even more.

And then one afternoon, when he arrived at the museum for a meeting, everything changed. She'd been flustered, out of sorts, not her usual calm and collected self. And then she'd turned, dragged him toward her by the collar and kissed him. Hotly. Frantically. As though it was the last thing in the world she wanted to do, but the one thing she *had* to do.

Within a week they were lovers, which had only intensified his desire to make her his own. And the more time they spent together and he got to know her, Liam's desire for Kayla turned into something else, something more and something that went way beyond physical attraction. Liam hadn't agreed with her insistence they remain secretive about their relationship, but he'd let her have her way at first, too crazy for her to deny her anything. But as the months slipped by he knew things had to change, particularly once they were married. He'd grown tired of sneaking around and pretending to their friends and family that they weren't together. She was his. He loved her and he wanted the world to know it.

"Liam, do you have a minute?"

He looked toward the open door. His assistant, Connie Bedford, stood in the doorway, wearing the skirt and jacket that was a signature of the hotel. Connie had worked at the hotel since she'd left high school, first on the front desk, and for the past few years as his administrative assistant. She was a sweet-natured young woman in her midtwenties who was hardworking, loyal and a godsend, and he always took note when she told him he was taking her for granted. She was also the only person who knew he was involved with Kayla, although she was too polite to ever mention it.

He beckoned her into the office. "Sure, what's up?"

Connie came into the room and dropped a few files on his desk. "I need some signatures," she explained and smiled. "And the new sous chef wants to see you today."

He groaned inwardly. Temperamental chefs were not on his radar when he was consumed with thoughts of his wife and the state of his marriage. But he still had a business to run and spent the next ten minutes with Connie, discussing a few issues regarding the hotel. By the time Connie left, his irritation had eased and he managed to get through the remainder of the afternoon without snapping the heads off any of the staff. The hotel ran 24/7, with twenty-two rooms over three floors, the restaurant and a bar, and two conference rooms that were regularly booked out. It employed over thirty-five locals on staff and was renowned for its comfort, ambience and service. Liam demanded nothing less and ran a tight ship.

There were several dude ranches just out of town that catered to big-city corporations wanting to use the experience as a bonding exercise for employees, or to city-dwellers longing for the typical *cowboy* experience. And since O'Sullivans was the best hotel within a hundred miles, it meant business was good. Better than good. The O'Sullivan coffers were compounding every day. He had wealth and success and a job that continued to be challenging, and the only thing missing from his life was a family of his own.

A wife. A child.

Kayla was his wife. And she might be carrying his child.

Longing, raw and intense, seeped through his blood. He'd never been in love before. He'd never experienced the heavy ache in his chest that he felt when he was away from her.

He'd lived an entitled life, one of wealth and of little struggle. The one painful point was his sister's death... Before that it had been easy street. But loving Kayla was changing him completely. He didn't want to upset her, hurt her or see her struggle with her divided loyalties... especially when he knew there was more pain to come. Despite their agreed-upon deadline for telling their parents their secret, ultimately he had no real idea what he would do when that time was up. Of course, he could tell his own parents first and then deal with the fallout, forcing Kayla into action. But he wasn't sure how he could do that without hurting the woman he loved.

Liam got to his feet and stretched his shoulders again. His office was on the second floor and from the long window behind his desk he had a view of the entire length of Main Street. The town, with its population of a few thousand, had one set of traffic lights, shop fronts that were both old and new, and well-maintained sidewalks. Until six months ago there had been two towns, separated by a river and a bridge. But after ten years of negotiating, the towns had merged, unified by the need to pool resources and create a stronger, more viable economy, taking advantage of commuters passing through the town on their way toward the state line. Cedar River was an old copper and silver mining town and Mount Rushmore and the Black Hills were within driving distance, so the town had plenty to offer tourists. The O'Sullivan portfolio of land and commercial property was vast, and Liam was proud of everything his father and grandfather had done since settling in the area sixty years earlier. His father, John-Dexter—or J.D. as he was known—had retired several years ago, handing the reins to Liam full-time, but still liked to show his face around the hotel. Liam didn't mind, since he got on well with his dad and hoped that one day he'd have a son or daughter who would follow in his own footsteps. That day suddenly seemed like a real possibility. And he was happy. Foolishly happy, despite the turmoil churning through his head.

His cell rang, cutting through his thoughts. It was his mother, reminding him that he'd agreed to meet with her to discuss several upcoming charitable events in town—including the hospital benefit that was being held at the art gallery in a couple of weeks. He'd been working on the project with Kayla, and not only would it raise much-needed funds for the hospital, but it would give several of the local artists an opportunity to showcase their work and he knew that it was important to her.

Liam shut down his laptop, grabbed his jacket and keys and headed downstairs to the foyer and reception desk. The restaurant and bar were off to the left and even though it was early, it looked like there was already a good crowd inside. There were other pubs in town, like Rusty's or the newly opened Loose Moose tavern. But O'Sullivan's was different—the modern decor was complemented by a traditional Irish feel and was accompanied by exemplary service and great food.

He spotted his mother the moment he stepped through the elevator. Gwen O'Sullivan was a tall, statuesque woman in her late fifties with short silvery hair and a timeless style she'd gained as a model in her youth. She was quiet and reserved, the total opposite of her blustery, well-meaning but often misunderstood husband. Liam knew he was more like his mother than his brothers. Sean, a movie producer in LA, was confident and brash and an admitted woman-izer. Liam doubted his youngest brother would ever settle down and ditch his fast life. Kieran, who was a doctor at a hospital in Sioux Falls, was a well-balanced sort of man with a positive outlook on pretty much everything, despite a messy divorce a year earlier. As he looked at his mother he was reminded of Liz, his sister, who'd died three years ago.

Liz and his mom had been close and he knew his mother grieved deeply for the daughter she'd lost. At times there was a hollowness to his mother's expression that seemed unable to be healed by anything, except perhaps the time she spent with her grandchildren, Liz's three young daugh-ters. But his sister's husband, Grady, had recently remar-ried and he knew his mother worried that she wouldn't see the girls as much. However, despite the fact that he'd never much liked Grady Parker and didn't believe the horse rancher was good enough for Liz, Liam had to admit that the other man was a caring father and tried to ensure his daughters maintained a relationship with Liz's family. It was complicated stuff. Made more so by the fact that Grady's new wife had been Liz's best friend since high school. Liam didn't believe anything had been going on before Liz's death, and he didn't really hold a grudge that Grady had moved on. He just…he just missed his sister. Liz had shown little interest in the O'Sullivan fortune or business and had thrived on her ranching life, her husband

and children. In a way, Liam had admired Liz for her steely determination to live her life exactly how she wanted.

"There you are," his mother said and greeted him with a brief hug. "Shall we talk over a drink?"

Liam checked his watch. Four forty. Not too early in the day, pushing down the niggling thought that his mother used alcohol to numb her pain at times. "Sure."

They headed into the bar and sat down at a booth. Liam ordered his mother a wine spritzer and a club soda with lime for himself. As much as he felt like getting wasted to get all thoughts of Kayla from his mind, the night manager didn't clock on until five and he had a strict rule about alcohol consumption while on duty.

"So," his mother said once their drinks arrived. "Do you want to tell me what's going on with you?"

Liam frowned. "I thought you wanted to talk about the charity schedule?"

"No," she said quietly. "That can wait. I want to talk about you. I'm worried about you."

Liam groaned inwardly. He should have seen this coming. Gwen O'Sullivan seemed to have some kind of built-in radar when it came to her offspring. The fact that Sean and Kieran lived elsewhere meant her attention was generally focused on him. Most days he could laugh it off, but today he wasn't in the mood for any kind of heart-to-heart with his well-meaning parent. "I'm fine."

She shook her head. "No, you're not. I know something's been bothering you."

"Stop smothering me, Mom," he said gently, not wanting to hurt her feelings. "I assure you, I'm fine."

She didn't look convinced, but smiled and drank some wine. Then she met his gaze levelly. "There's more to life than work, you know. More to life than this hotel."

Liam raised a brow. "Tell that to Dad."

"At least your father took the time to get married and raise a family," she reminded him. "Unlike you and your brothers. When Kieran got married I thought that at least one of my boys had the good sense to settle down. But then there was that awful divorce and everything else. And Sean just moves from one flighty woman to the next. And then there's you…my sensible son, who doesn't let anyone in."

It wasn't true. He'd let Kayla in. Into his life and into his heart. Unfortunately, most days he felt as though she was walking all over it. Liam sat back in his seat and half smiled. "You know, I think we have this same conversation every six months or so."

"Then it's time you took notice," she said, still frowning. "You're nearly thirty-five years old. It's time you settled down, got married and had children. We need grand-children to carry on the family name, after all. And as much as I love them, your sister's children are Parkers, not O'Sullivans. You're not even dating anyone at the moment."

"Mother," he said as gently as he could, because in his heart he knew that despite her calm, sometimes controlled ways, there was a frailty to Gwen O'Sullivan that only a few people saw. "It's not the kind of thing that is made to order, you know."

"Of course it is," she said and smiled. "Do you think I had any say in the matter when your father courted me?"

He grinned. "Knowing Dad, probably not."

"What about Abby Perkins?" she suggested as both brows shot up. "She's a nice woman. And very pretty."

Abby was the head chef at O'Sullivan's. "Mom, I—"

"It's a shame that Lucy Monero is engaged to that Parker boy. Now, she would have been a great match for you. And she's a doctor. And she's got such beautiful hair."

Liam zoned out as his mother prattled on about Lucy Monero, who was a doctor at the local hospital and was soon to marry Grady Parker's younger brother. She was also one of Kayla's closest friends.

Liam drank the club soda and vaguely listened as his mother kept talking and mentioning several single women that he knew between the ages of twenty and forty.

"What about Ash McCune?" she asked.

Ash was another friend of Kayla's, a pretty redhead and a police officer. "Not my type," he said and grinned.

His mother scowled. "Ellie Culhane?"

"Too young."

"Carmel Morrissey."

He grinned. "Too old."

Liam could see his mother thinking about other potential would-be wives and he drew in a long breath. He knew she was clucking around him to keep her thoughts off losing her only daughter and he wasn't about to be unkind and tell her to stop. As much as her matchmaking got on his nerves, he would never intentionally hurt her feelings. She was his mother, and that alone was enough of a reason to bite his tongue.

Besides, there was a certain irony in the conversation. His mother was urging him to get married and start a family. He was almost tempted to say he'd already done that. But he wouldn't say anything until they knew for sure.

The concierge approached, interrupting them about a problem with a guest. Liam held on to his patience as the younger man explained the issue and then barked out a couple of instructions. Some days he longed for a solitary job where he didn't have staff lining up with questions. He almost envied Kayla her isolation at the museum. When the other man left them, Liam noticed his mother watching him, both brows up.

"What?" he said.

"No one likes a bad-tempered boss," she said and grinned.

"I don't have a bad temper."

"Well, not with me you don't," she said and patted his arm. "And you're very sweet with your nieces and little old ladies and I'm proud of the way you've taken Connie under your wing these past few years. But with the rest of the world, including the people who work for you, you seem to have developed a reputation for being grumpy and impatient."

The criticism irked him more than usual. "Because I like things done a certain way?"

"Because you like things done *your* way," she replied and patted his arm again. "You know, you really do seem tense. I think you need to loosen up a bit."

"I'm loose enough," he said, even though he knew people believed he was uptight most of the time. It was who he was, who he'd always been. He was J.D. O'Sullivan's eldest son, heir and successor to the O'Sullivan legacy... imagining he could have had any other kind of life was never an option. Not that he'd had any real ambition to do anything else. Unlike Kieran who'd always known his path was medicine, or Sean, who wanted a faster paced life than small town, South Dakota.

Still, he couldn't help but sometimes wonder what would have happened if he'd changed course after college, maybe focused on the photography that he'd loved in his teens. But it was all rather moot now... He ran the hotel and the O'Sullivan portfolio and had a responsibility to his family and the many employees who relied on O'Sullivan's for their livelihood.

"Liam?"

His mother's voice got his mind back on track. "Yes?"

"What about Annie Jamison or—"

"Enough," he said gently and held his palm up. "Okay, Mom, I get the drift. You want me to get married and then have a few sons so we can carry on the great O'Sullivan name." He got to his feet and pushed in the chair. "I'll do my best not to disappoint you or Dad."

"You never disappoint us. Not ever."

He tried not to, although he knew that when the truth about his relationship with Kayla came out, there would be disappointment on both sides. It was inevitable. But something had to give. At the very least Kayla needed to meet him halfway. With his mother trying to marry him off, it wouldn't be long before Gwen O'Sullivan worked out why he was reluctant to date anyone, let alone anything more.

Liam stood, grabbed his jacket and keys, said goodbye to his mother and left. He needed to talk to his wife. Right now. It couldn't wait.

By the time Kayla got to her apartment that afternoon it was after five o'clock. She pulled up outside the old Victorian that she'd called home for nearly a year. The big house had been renovated into four apartments and Kayla's was on the second floor.

She loved the house, with its textured cladding, shuttered windows and wide-front veranda. The home had been carefully restored by the owner, an IT guru who'd inherited the place a few years earlier from an elderly relative he'd never met. Dane was something of a geeky recluse, but he was a good landlord and neighbor. Even though he was a couple of years younger than Kayla they had formed a solid friendship over the past year, and with the married couple in their midforties sharing one of the downstairs apartments and the other occupied by a seventysomething widow, she was grateful to have such caring neighbors and friends.

When Ash arrived just after five thirty, still in her police officer's uniform, Kayla offered her tea and within ten minutes they were sitting on the sofa, the flyers for the upcoming hospital benefit spread on the coffee table between them.

"They look great," Kayla said and nodded. "Thank you for doing this. I know how busy you are. But this is exactly what I was envisioning."

"The kids had fun with the design," Ash said and smiled. "They incorporated the hospital logo, but still made them fun and colorful."

Kayla looked at her friend. Not only was Ash a single mother and a police officer, she was also a foster parent. She was probably the most generous and giving person that Kayla knew. On her small ranch just out of town, she took in teens who needed a helping hand, sometimes several at the same time. She lived on the ranch with her mother, Nancy, and her twelve-year-old son, Jaye.

"Thank you," Kayla said again and sighed. "I really appreciate your help."

"That's what friends are for," Ash reminded her. "Right?"

Kayla dropped her gaze. Ash was astute. And she knew her friend sensed something wasn't quite right with her. "Yes…absolutely."

"Does that mean you want to talk about you know who?"

Her friends had all been nagging her about her relationship with Liam since the night she'd plowed into his truck, but none of them knew for certain they were involved. When they suggested it, Kayla generally laughed it off. But tonight, she wasn't in the mood for laughing. When they discovered she was Liam's wife she would have a lot of explaining to do.

Liam's wife.

Sometimes she could barely get her head around it. They'd met up in Vegas the day her conference had ended and spent three days together. The most amazing three days of her life. And they'd returned as husband and wife. It had been a foolish, spur-of-the-moment decision. A monumental decision. If she'd had any sense she would have had the marriage annulled. But she was all out of sense when it came to Liam. And since the idea of ending their relationship hurt her through to her bones, she felt as though she was in an impossible position. Hurt herself and Liam *and* the child she was possibly carrying…or hurt her parents and grandmother.

Either way, it was a disaster waiting to happen.

And although she didn't like the way they'd ended their telephone call earlier that afternoon, she was too tired to ring him back and go over the same old ground. She knew what he wanted…and on one level she agreed with him. She simply didn't know how to give it to him without hurting the people who loved her most in the world.

Of course a baby would change everything. Her child would come first, there was no question about that. She simply wasn't going to be in some great hurry to tell everyone.

"No," Kayla said to her friend. "I'm not up for that… not just yet."

Ash sighed and offered a gentle smile. "I know what it is to feel trapped by…" Her friend's words trailed off before she spoke again. "By obligation. But when you're ready, you know I'm on hand to listen."

Ash was a good friend and had been through a lot over the years, particularly when it came to her young son and ex-fiancé. And Kayla knew her friend understood loyalty and family commitment. If she was going to unburden herself, she would be exactly who Kayla would talk to. With Lucy and Brooke so blissfully in love these days, Ash was the only one of her friends who would understand what she was feeling.

There was a knock on the door, so Kayla excused herself, got to her feet and headed down the short hallway. Thinking it might be Lucy or Brooke or even Dane stopping by for a chat, she swung the door back on its hinges and smiled. But it wasn't one of her friends on her doorstep.

It was her husband.

Her gaze was instinctively drawn to his broad shoulders. How many times had she rested her head there? How many times had she gripped his arms and back and every other part of him. Countless. For the past five months they had shared a bed and she'd been privy to the real Liam O'Sullivan. Not the arrogant and indifferent man he was thought to be. She'd seen his other side…the tender and passionate man who always talked to her softly after they'd made love. The man who was generous and kind and adored his nieces. The man who teased her about her bad cooking. The man who made her mindless and breathless with just the barest kiss.

"Liam," she whispered the word as though it was her last. "What are you doing here?"

He still wore his suit, so he had obviously come directly from the hotel. "You didn't text me," he said flatly. "And I wanted to see you."

Kayla glanced over her shoulder. "Ash is here," she said quietly. "So it's not a good time to have a—"

"Ash is just leaving," her friend's mellow voice announced as she made her way up the hall. "Hi there, Liam," Ash then said cheerfully. "Good to see you. I'll talk with you soon," the other woman said and gave Kayla a brief hug. "About *everything*," Ash whispered close to her ear before she brushed past Liam and headed through the door.

Once her friend had disappeared down the stairs, Kayla turned her attention to Liam. "Really?"

He half shrugged. "What?"

She glared at him. "Since when do you turn up here unannounced?"

"Beats waiting for an invitation," he said as he crossed the threshold and walked down the hall.

Annoyance snaked up her spine as she followed him into the living room. "We talked about this, Liam. I told you Ash was going to be—"

"We talked about a lot of things," he said, terser than usual, his blue eyes so dark they were almost black. He stood by the sofa, hitched his hands on his hips and stared at her. "And yet, here we are...no closer to sorting it out."

"Did you come here just to rehash the same old argument?"

He stilled, his jaw clenched and then he exhaled heavily. "I came here to see you. To talk to you. To *be* with you."

Shame pressed down on her shoulders. Of course he'd want to talk. And she did, too. "I'm sorry... I know this must be hard for you, too. But we both know this situation can't be resolved easily. At least not without a whole lot of people getting hurt."

He met her gaze. "People get hurt, Kayla. Sometimes there's nothing you can do to stop that."

She swallowed hard. "I can. I have to try... I can't simply—"

"Please come home with me tonight," he said, cutting her off, his voice raw. "You've spent the last five nights at your apartment. You spent three nights here last week. It's becoming something of a habit. And I...I miss you."

She blinked at his honest admission. "I miss you, too. But..."

He let out an impatient sigh. "But obviously not enough to come home?"

Home?

His home. Technically her home, too...but she could never quite bring herself to say it out loud. "With Ash stopping by to show me the flyers for the benefit it was just easier to stay at the apartment to avoid too many questions."

He shrugged loosely. "I know how much the museum means to you Kayla…and I support your work and all you do and how passionate you are about the hospital benefit. But I don't want to get used to sleeping alone."

Her back straightened. "So this is about sex?"

His gaze narrowed instantly. "What?"

"Sex," she said again. "You know, that thing we do when we're together."

"This isn't about sex," he assured her, his voice so husky it warmed her through to her bones. "It's about you and me. It's about our relationship…our marriage. And we can't have a marriage if you're holed up here in your old apartment every chance you get."

It was the same old song. Her apartment. His house by the river. Kayla had been dividing herself between the two places for months. More so since their spur-of-the-moment wedding. "We've been through this before, Liam. You know how I feel and I can't simply switch myself off from the rest of my life." Emotion thickened her throat. "I know what you want from me, but I can't break my father's heart because it suits me to do so."

"Are you so sure that you will?"

"Yes," she shot back quickly. "I know my father. And I know he will have trouble accepting this…accepting you… accepting *us*. You're J.D. O'Sullivan's son and I'm Derek Rickard's daughter. In his eyes it will be…*impossible*."

He frowned a little. "Nonetheless, it's a fact. One that can't be avoided forever."

"I can't do it," she insisted. "Not yet. I know I said I would…but I need more time, especially now that I'm possibly pregnant. You know my grandmother hasn't been well and I don't want to make things worse for my parents. Not right now. Please try to understand."

Thinking about her ailing grandmother made her ache inside. She loved her family dearly. But she loved Liam, too. And to her parents it would be seen as the worst kind of betrayal.

But if there is a baby...

She would have to tell them. She would have to choose. Liam and her child, or her parents and her child. It was untenable. Unthinkable.

"Then, when?" he asked, clearly stuck on the idea. "When our kid is twenty-one?"

Kayla met his eyes and watched as his expression shifted. She recognized the way his strong jaw was suddenly tense and his shoulders twitched. He was mad. With her. At her. And obviously in spite of himself because Liam rarely let anyone witness his moods.

"You're being impossible," she said hotly and then shrugged, knowing it would inflame him, but she wasn't about to start appeasing his moods.

"Once you start showing you won't have anything to hide behind," he shot back. "Unless you plan on saying the baby is someone else's."

Irritation curled up her spine. "Of course I don't. And I'm not hiding," she refuted. "Frankly, I don't understand this sudden need to announce our relationship to the world," she said and raised both brows. "Unless you want to deliberately stick it to *your* father, because let's be honest— he won't be any happier about this than my dad will be."

He stayed perfectly still. "My father has nothing to do with this. Neither should yours."

That was where they differed, she thought hotly. "Perhaps I'm not as good at trampling over people's feelings as you are."

"Really?" he fired back, his blue eyes glittering. "Because you seem to do a damned fine job of trampling over mine!"

There it was. Out in the open. Exactly what he believed.

Emotion clutched at her throat. Kayla hadn't planned on crying, but tears filled her eyes just the same. She blinked, forcing back the heat behind her eyes, and then swallowed hard. He saw it all and within seconds was in front of her. He reached out to touch her, but she stepped back, her legs colliding with the edge of the sofa as she folded her arms tightly.

"Kayla…" He said her name, quieter now, his anger quickly defused. "I'm sorry. I didn't mean to shout at you. I'm just so…" His words trailed off as he ran a hand through his hair. "I'm just really…"

Kayla knew exactly what he was. Frustrated. Annoyed. And impatient.

With good reason…

Logically, she knew he had every right to be angry. But when it came to hurting her parents, logic flew out the window. "You should go," she said flatly. "I'll see you in the morning."

He sighed heavily. "Is this really how you want to leave things tonight?"

She shrugged. "I don't have the energy for another argument."

He winced, like she'd struck a nerve. Then he reached out to cup her cheek. Kayla pulled back instinctively and he frowned as he dropped his hand. "Okay, I'll leave you alone. Good night, Kayla."

"Good night."

Any other time he would have passionately kissed her good-night. Held her and touched her a while before he left. And she would have let him. But tonight felt different.

There was more tension than usual between them. More unsaid words. More distance.

Then he was gone. Out of the apartment. Out of the building. And Kayla didn't take a breath until she heard his footsteps going down the stairs.

Chapter Three

Alone in his bed hours after he walked out of Kayla's apartment, Liam spent most of the night staring at the ceiling and twisting in sheets, longing for Kayla's body beside him. The scent of her perfume seemed to haunt him like a ghost, reminding him that it had been close to a week since they'd spent the night under the same roof.

The huge, Western red cedar house seemed unusually quiet and all he could hear was the familiar sound of the river nearby and the rhythmic chorus of insects in the trees. He had the house built a couple of years ago on a three-acre block that was mostly forest and very private, with a long gravel driveway that was plowed regularly in the snow season. There was a stone path leading to the river and a jetty where he kept his pair of Jet Skis; the boat he was re-building was in the boathouse.

He sighed, opening his eyes, and then looked directly out the open window. The moonlight filtered light across the river and the water was eerily luminescent. From the roomy loft-style main bedroom he had a great view of the river. On warm summer nights he mostly left the window open and enjoyed the breeze that swept through the upper level. Liam inhaled deeply and the scent of jasmine in the air reminded him of Kayla.

Everything reminded him of Kayla.

The air, the sheets...every damned thing.

His gut was in knots. Today they would find out if she was pregnant. The idea intensified his love for her tenfold. He wanted children and he wanted them with her. He knew what this would do to her family and perhaps his own. But with the idea that they were going to be parents now firmly etched into his mind, Liam didn't care. They would have to deal with it, or deal out. Kayla and the baby she might be carrying were the only things that mattered.

He closed his eyes and imagined her belly round with his child. Her beauty would be amplified, her skin would glow, her breasts would be fuller. Then he remembered her pale, smooth skin and her perfect breasts and how they'd fit in his hands, and immediately his palms itched and his groin ached.

Liam groaned, sat up and swung his legs off the side of the big bed. He checked the clock on the bedside table. Three fifteen. He grabbed his phone and stood, pulling on a pair of sweats and a T-shirt, and then headed downstairs.

The cat, a scruffy-looking black-and-white stray he'd randomly named Peanuts, which had turned up on his doorstep the week after he'd moved in, began meowing the moment he was spotted on the stairs. The cat always slept in a basket by the big fireplace, summer or winter. Liam had no real feelings about the feline one way or another. But he kept it fed and housed and had even installed a cat flap in the back door so it could come and go as it pleased. It did seem to stay more than leave, no doubt due to the comfy bed and endless supply of kibble.

He flicked on a couple of lights and headed for the huge galley-style kitchen. The Shaker-style cupboards were crafted from local ponderosa pine and the countertops were dark gray marble. The double ceramic sink and stainless-steel appliances were all top-of-the-line and mostly imported. Like with everything in the home, no expense was spared. From the cedar floorboards, Spanish-glass light fittings and handcrafted furniture, it was a showpiece. But Liam had no illusions—it was a house, not a home.

It needed a family in it. When Kayla was there it felt full, complete and real. When she wasn't, there was only him, using the bare minimum of the rooms, just the kitchen and den, main bedroom and bathroom. There were three other bedrooms downstairs and a media room and a small home office. He'd built a house for a family he didn't have, imagining that one day he'd fill it with a wife and a few children. That had been his plan a year ago... He'd intended to find a suitable woman and settle down. And then a certain blonde had crashed into his car and completely derailed his life.

She was so beautiful. Tall and slender, but surprisingly curvy, with a glorious mane of golden blond hair she rarely allowed anyone to see styled in anything other than a tightly coiled bun. But Liam had seen it out and falling down the length of her back countless times. He'd fisted handfuls of her tresses to expose her perfectly smooth throat. He'd run his hands through her hair as they'd lain together on the big bed upstairs, intimately entwined, unsure where one began and the other finished, kissing and touching and making love.

He shook off the memory and made green tea. Another habit from his five-month relationship with Kayla. She was a strict vegetarian and believed in healthy eating, admonishing his proclivity for strong black coffee and leftover pizza for breakfast. It made him smile and he sipped the tea as he headed for the living room.

The cat was still meowing and began curling around his ankles. He gave the animal a pat, drank some more tea and dropped into one of the big leather sofas, then stared at the cold fireplace. In winter the room was cozy, despite its size. Liam placed the tea on the side table, relaxed his head against the leather and closed his eyes.

And didn't wake up until seven thirty.

By ten past eight he was showered and dressed, and was turning the ignition in the Silverado.

He made a call to Connie at the hotel saying he wouldn't be in until the afternoon, ignoring the question about his whereabouts, and then headed off down the driveway. He pulled up outside Kayla's apartment at eight twenty-five and spotted her by the front door before he had a chance to shut down the truck. A man was with her and Liam instinctively scowled. Her landlord. He was a lanky, disheveled looking geek who he'd spoken to a couple of times and didn't like one bit. In his opinion the other guy was a little too friendly toward Kayla. He put the vehicle in Park and got out, striding around the other side as she waved goodbye to the other man and then made her way down the paved path. She looked tired and he figured she'd probably had as little sleep as he had. She wore a pale blue dress that buttoned high up the front and fell just above her knees and made her long legs look sensational. He experienced the usual ripple of attraction that wound its way up his spine. He smiled when she reached the vehicle.

"Good morning," he said easily. "Sleep okay?"

"Like a log," she replied and they both knew she was lying through her teeth.

They'd parted badly the night before. He'd lost his temper with her, something he loathed doing. "I'm sorry about last night… I should have called first. Or I should have—"

"Forget about it," she said quietly. "Let's just get this done. So, how did you sleep?" she asked as he opened the passenger door.

"Barely a wink," he said as she got into the truck.

Once he was back in the driver's seat she spoke again. "I woke up at about quarter past three."

As he did. "Me, too," he admitted. "Although I did manage to catch another few hours on the couch."

"You're lucky. But my couch isn't as comfortable as yours."

He recalled her lumpy sofa that she'd picked up at a yard sale. She loved antiquities and old wares and her home was spotted with pieces of furniture she'd salvaged and restored. He'd never done any sleeping on her couch, but they'd done a whole lot of loving.

"If I recall correctly you have a comfortable bed."

Color pinched her cheeks. After everything they had been to one another, she still blushed around him. "Comfy enough," she said and clutched the tote she carried. "We should get going."

"Not yet," he said and wound his hand around her nape and drew her close.

"What are you doing?" she asked, pulling back a little.

"Kissing my wife," he replied and claimed her lips possessively.

It took about three seconds for her to respond and Liam smiled against her mouth. They could fight. They could disagree. They could spend time apart. She could give him every excuse under the sun as to how difficult it was for them to be together. But the attraction and feeling between them was undeniable. Her lips parted invitingly and he deepened the kiss, slanting his mouth over her own, finding her tongue and drawing it gently between his teeth. Kissing Kayla was like trying to quench a thirst…it was never enough, never deep enough, never hot enough, never intense enough.

"Liam," she said breathlessly, suddenly dragging her lips from his. "Would you please stop? Someone could see us and—"

"Like who?" he demanded and threaded his fingers through her hair. "Your neighbors? Your geeky landlord, who I'm pretty sure has got the hots for you?"

She pulled away and straightened in the seat. "That's ridiculous. Dane is my friend, that's all."

Liam settled in front of the steering wheel and strapped on the seat belt. "I still don't like him."

Kayla huffed out a breath. "Would you stop acting like a jealous—"

"A jealous husband?" Liam shot back, cutting her off as he started the engine. "That's what I am, remember? *Your husband.*"

She pulled her tote onto her lap. "I know who and what you are. And I know that since the moment I told you I might be pregnant you've been behaving like a real jerk."

Kayla was mad. Things were complicated enough without Liam making it worse by having some kind of macho freak-out about her landlord. She glared at him and then turned her head to stare out of the front window. It wasn't the first time he'd mentioned he thought Dane had a crush on her, although she'd always laughed it off before. But not today. She was too wound up to find the humor in his words.

She glanced at his left hand and noticed he was wearing his wedding ring, while her own finger felt shamefully bare. The platinum-and-diamond band was in her purse, wrapped in a tissue and tucked away for safekeeping. But Liam always seemed to wear his when they were alone together. It irked her a little. And guilted her, too. He acted more like a husband than she did a wife.

Deep down, she knew all his arguments about telling their parents—especially now—were right. But she couldn't get over her fear that it would be like adding one final splash of gasoline to the pile of wood. And that news of a Rickard-O'Sullivan pregnancy would hardly do anything to defuse that blast. She'd been awake all night worrying—

"Is there any place in particular you'd like to go?" he asked, his voice jerking her back into the present. "Maybe try to get in to see a doctor?"

Her head snapped sideways. "No doctors. Just a drugstore. If the result is positive from the test then I'll go and see my own physician once…once…you know…"

"Once the truth is out, you mean," he said quietly and then glanced at her stomach. "So…how far along do you think you are?"

She shrugged. "I don't know. Over a month. Maybe two."

He was silent for a moment, and then spoke. "We've always used contraception."

Kayla had wondered when that statement would rear its head. "Condoms are only ninety-eight percent effective."

"Really?"

"Yes," she replied and smiled sweetly. "Haven't you ever read the packet?"

He laughed and the sound affected her way down. Sometimes, she couldn't believe he could still do that, that she could be as gushy and as aware of him as though they were on a first date. Her lips tingled when she remembered how possessively he'd kissed her only minutes earlier.

"I've never been one for reading the instructions," he said softly.

"Or taking them," she said and folded her arms. "But you do like to boss everyone else around."

He laughed again. "I've missed this."

"Missed what?"

"You listing all my faults," he said and grinned. "I guess I have a few."

"No," she replied and smiled. "Not too many at all. Which is really annoying," she said and smiled a little. The levity between them was a welcome change, but Kayla wasn't fooled. He was as wound up as she was. She noticed his hands were tight on the steering wheel and a pulse throbbed in his cheek. "You know, if you grip that steering wheel any tighter your knuckles might crack."

He glanced at her and then relaxed his hands fractionally. "Coping mechanism."

She chuckled softly. "You're such a fraud, Liam."

His jaw tensed even further. "What does that mean?"

She looked at him for a moment, fiddling with the strap on her tote, then returned her gaze straight ahead. "Tough guy. Calm, cool and collected. Ice in your veins. You know, all the things people say about you. None of it's really true."

"Sure it is," he said dismissively.

"Yesterday I thought you were all in control and ready for whatever happened today," she said, smiling again. "But I think you're as nervous as I am. Maybe even more so. Let's face it, your family is going to be as shocked about this as mine. And equally disapproving."

"As I said last night, I don't actually care about that, Kayla," he said flatly. "I care about you and the child you might be carrying. You make a baby with someone, then you take on the responsibility that goes with it."

"And to hell with everything else?" she shot back. "And *everyone* else?"

"Precisely."

"I can't disregard other people's feelings like that."

His mouth flattened. "Really?"

She sighed with frustration. "I don't disregard *your* feelings, Liam. At least, I don't set out to do that. But we both knew going into this relationship that it wasn't going to be easy, considering our history."

"Our history?" he echoed. "But we didn't have a history, Kayla. It was our parents' history, our parents' private war, for want of a better expression. We were both raised on a steady diet of hatred for each other's family. And in one way or another, if you are pregnant, then this child will end that cycle. We have to make sure of that. Otherwise, our parents won't have the opportunity to be a part of this child's life."

"That sounds all very cut-and-dried," she remarked. "But we both know I could never cut my parents out of their grandchild's life...and I don't think you could, either."

"I'll do what I have to do to protect my family," he said and the words chilled her a little. She knew he would do exactly as he said. "My *family*. You and me. And you'll do the same."

Kayla crossed her arms and sucked in a deep breath. "For you to say that to me it's obvious that you don't know me at all."

"Of course I know you," he said quietly. "I know every inch of you...intimately."

"Sex and intimacy are two very different things."

He laughed humorlessly. "Ain't that the truth."

Kayla hung on to her temper and barely spoke for the remainder of the trip. He was being a hothead for reasons of his own. Thankfully they'd reached Rapid City and once they entered the town precinct she began scouring the streets for the first open drugstore she could find. They found a mall quickly and once he'd parked the truck she got out and shut the door, not waiting for him as she walked across the parking lot. He caught up soon enough and they walked side by side into the store. To his credit he hung back while she made her selection and didn't do his usual thing of insisting on paying for everything.

For all his faults, she couldn't accuse him of being anything other than incredibly generous. His benevolence didn't stop with the museum and she knew he was generous toward the local hospital's charitable work and fundraising. Despite his reputation for being a ruthless, arrogant and entitled alpha male, he had a kind and giving spirit that she'd been privy to during their time together.

"All done?" he asked once she'd paid the clerk and had the parcel in her hands. She nodded and he then did the same. "So, we could go for coffee somewhere in town. There's that little café on Omaha Street that you like. You know, the place with the pistachio brownies."

Kayla was instantly bombarded with a memory. It was a week after that crazy afternoon at the museum when she'd given in to the constant battle of trying to resist her attraction to him and had kissed him madly. They'd spent the day in Rapid City and she'd discovered his addiction to caffeinated beverages as they frequented several cafés in search of the perfect cup. They had a lovely afternoon together and later that evening he booked them into a luxury hotel, where they ordered room service and then made love for the first time. The following morning they had a late breakfast at the café on Omaha Street and Kayla had stocked up on the delicious brownies. It seemed so long ago now, and not five short months earlier. But the memories were acute.

"I'd prefer to go back home and get this done," she said

and rattled the paper bag in her hand. "No point in putting off the inevitable."

He took his time to agree, but eventually they were on their way back down the highway after stopping to refuel at a gas station. The trip home was mainly done in silence. A heavy band of tension pressed down on her temples and she was suddenly weary. Her lack of sleep the night before took its toll and it didn't take long for her eyes to close.

Being jostled on a bumpy road snapped her out of sleep and she opened her eyes and blinked a couple of times. Tall trees and a huge timber house loomed ahead. Liam's place. *Their place.* She knew the road and the house well. It was secluded and private and just the place for a secret relationship.

"I thought you'd prefer it," he said as an explanation. "No prying eyes."

It was another dig about her nosey neighbors, but she ignored it, figuring it didn't matter where she took the test. Kayla grabbed her tote and got out of the truck the moment he pulled up outside the house. It was a warm day and the river was flat and shimmering beneath the midday sun. It was such a beautiful spot, perhaps the best along the river, and the house was incredible. Two and a half levels of understated opulence, the finest red cedar partnered with perfect architecture that took full advantage of sunlight and breeze and was well shielded by trees in the winter months.

They headed inside and Kayla's heels clicked over the polished floor as she walked down the hall. Peanuts came scampering toward her and she bent down to pet the cat for a moment. The familiarity of the house wrapped around her as she moved into the living room. The fireplace, the bare mantel and the thick hearth rug where she'd lain with Liam countless times quickly reminded her of how little time she'd spent at the house recently.

"Are you okay?"

His voice.

It was like liquid being poured down her spine. She turned and noticed he was barely a few feet from her. "Fine."

"You're nervous," he said and stepped closer, grasping her hand.

His touch.

She could barely think straight when his skin connected with hers. Kayla looked to where their hands were linked and every impulse she had urged her to pull away. "I'm not sure how I feel."

He dropped his hand and her palm felt acutely empty. He was looking at her oddly, not angrily, not unhappily... more like he was confused.

"You know, a baby isn't the end of the world, Kayla. Babies are a precious gift."

Of course their baby would be a gift. "I know that. I *feel* that. If I'm pregnant I will love this baby and cherish it and be there for him or her, always." Heat burned her eyes. "I know the baby will come first, I know logically that nothing else can matter. But that doesn't stop me from being torn up inside knowing how this will kill my father." Her voice shook with emotion, and she knew Liam saw the true fear beneath her stubbornness—the fear of a daughter about to hurt her daddy. She couldn't hide it. Or deceive him. Because he knew her, better than anyone else.

"No, it won't," he assured her gently. "Sure, your dad will be mad and maybe he'll be disappointed. But at the end of the day, we're talking about his grandchild. Perhaps you need to give your parents a little more credit than imagining they're going to be outraged."

She wasn't convinced. "You don't know them."

"True. But they love you, Kayla. You're their only child, they're not going to disown you over this."

He didn't understand. She loved her parents, and she knew they loved her. But she knew that despite his confidence, this would break their hearts, particularly her father's.

She wiped her eyes. "I'm going to take the test."

He nodded. "I'll make you some tea if you like."

"Sure," she said and grabbed her bag.

Kayla turned and headed for the stairs, climbing them slowly, each step excruciating, and knowing he was watching her only amplified her anxiety. She entered the bedroom and looked at the king-size bed and the dark blue quilt that seemed so familiar to her. She looked at the bedside table and spotted her tortoiseshell hair clip, still lying where she'd left it a week earlier. Her nightgown lay at the foot of the bed and her favorite scuffs were by the nightstand.

She ignored the fluttering in her belly, dropped her tote by the bed and headed for the bathroom, closing the door. The huge black marble and white tiled room afforded every spa-like luxury. There was a whirlpool bath in one corner and a large double shower in the other.

She unwrapped the pregnancy test, pulled out the instructions, set the box on the sink and stepped back. She read the words quickly. Pee on the stick. One line equals not pregnant. Two lines equals pregnant.

Easy.

I can do this.

She followed the instructions and then placed the stick onto the vanity before she sat on the edge of the tub and waited, eyes closed, her hands clasped together. Then she opened her eyes, managed the few steps toward the sink, took a long breath and stared at the two blue lines on the stick.

Realization quickly dawned.

Two lines equals pregnant.

She took a moment and sucked in another breath. And

another, allowing the realization to spread across her skin and then seep through to her bones. She was light-headed, shocked, and then slowly the shock subsided and something else took over. Love, uncomplicated and raw and breath-takingly powerful, suddenly surged through her. And she knew instantly what it was.

A mother's love.

A feeling like no other. Kayla rubbed her belly with her palm.

Hi there, I'm your Mommy. And nothing else matters now...just you.

Heat burned her eyes and she swallowed the lump in her throat as she snatched up the stick. Suddenly and with life-altering clarity, Kayla knew that loving and protecting her baby was all that mattered. And she would do whatever she had to do to ensure that her child was safe and loved. She took another breath, opened the door and headed back downstairs.

Liam was in the kitchen making tea. She watched him from the doorway, so handsome in his jeans and navy polo shirt. There was something effortlessly masculine about the way he moved, the way he carried out even the most mundane task. His arms were well-defined and muscular, his hands strong and perfectly sculptured. He was as comfortable indoors as he was out. She'd witnessed the way he seamlessly ran the hotel, but she'd also seen him outside, building fences, chopping firewood, repairing the boat in the boathouse. He was one of those people who mastered everything he touched.

Including me...

He was a passionate and demanding man, but equally gentle and generous. There was tenderness, too. Long nights where they would spend time talking, whispering, sharing their deepest thoughts as though there was no one else in the world, no one to intrude, no one to break the spell.

Her hand rested instinctively on her belly. They shared a child now. A life. And would be bound together forever. Would their baby inherit Liam's blue eyes and strong jaw? Would he or she be golden- or dark-haired? Would their baby share Liam's confidence and generosity, or be caring and cautious, like she was. Either way, one huge question kept slamming around in her head. How were they going to do this without hurting everyone who loved them?

They couldn't. People *would* be hurt. Choices would have to be made. Alliances and loyalties would be stretched. It was a lose-lose situation.

Babies are a precious gift...

His words echoed in her mind.

Their baby.

Five minutes ago it was a possibility. Now it was a reality. The baby she carried *was* a precious gift...and she would guard that gift with every fiber of her being. She knew what it meant. She knew what he would want. Maybe even demand. She could feel it coming with each passing second.

"Liam?"

He looked up and stilled, ditching the mugs to stand at the end of the counter. He looked tense, as on edge as she'd ever seen him. "Hey."

Kayla stepped farther into the room, swallowing the tension rising in her throat. She clutched the end of the testing stick and held it by her side as she met his querying gaze. His eyes had never seemed bluer, his expression never more intense.

She took a few steps closer and waited for him to move. But he stayed where he was, clearly letting her choose the pace of the conversation. So like him, she thought. His strength was listening, despite what people believed about him. Sometimes he said very little. Sometimes he would hold her and let her ramble on about her family and her work and just smile that wry smile of his, absorbing every word she spoke.

Kayla took the last few steps, reached the counter and wordlessly placed the test on the marble top. He stared at it for several seconds and then met her gaze.

"What…" The word almost sounded strangled and then she watched, fascinated as he swallowed hard and placed his hands on the counter. "What does it mean?"

"Two lines," she whispered. "Two lines means positive."

He was standing so still he looked as though he'd been carved from stone. His palms were flat on the counter, his shoulders a hard line, his jaw so incredibly tight she fought the urge to touch his face.

"You're really pregnant?"

She nodded. "Yes."

"A baby…really…" His voice trailed off, as though he was trying to make sense of it, trying to absorb the idea through to his skin and bones and blood. He drew in a long breath. Then another. His gaze unwavering as he locked it with hers, packed with raw, unparalleled emotion.

"We're really having a baby," she said, the words almost on a sigh.

She watched as his throat closed over, mesmerized by the sheer intensity of his reaction. There was nothing stoic or controlled about Liam O'Sullivan in that moment. He was all vulnerability, all feeling, and clearly as overwhelmed by the idea of being a parent as she was.

He took a couple of strides toward her and then she was against him, his arms strong and safe as they wound around her and held her firm. She felt him tremble, heard his heart thundering behind his ribs as her head nestled into his chest. Kayla could barely breathe, barely think…only *feel*. It was exactly how she'd imagined the moment would be. With emotion. With intimacy. With love. The connection between them ran deeper than any other moment ever had. And she knew he felt it as intensely as she did.

He kissed the top of her head and she swayed against him. And finally, when he spoke again, his voice wound up her spine and through her blood.

"We should go and tell your parents. And then mine. Right now."

Kayla pulled back instantly and put space between them. She stared at him, feeling her temper begin to rise. It wasn't unusual for Liam to be domineering and bossy—he just generally didn't do that with her. But he could be as bossy as he liked, she wasn't giving in.

"No," she said quietly.

He moved around the counter. "No?"

Kayla stood her ground. "I *will* tell my parents, Liam. But not yet."

"When?"

"When I'm ready."

"This isn't just your decision," he said tightly. "Not now."

"Nor yours," she reminded him.

Gridlock.

He sucked in a long breath, pulled his cell phone from his pocket and held it out toward her. "Call your folks… or I will."

Kayla glared at him. Perhaps he would never understand. Perhaps she'd been deluded all along. Maybe it wasn't in his makeup to feel a sense of duty toward family. Oh, he knew a lot about responsibility—he'd shown that for years at the helm of the hotel and the O'Sullivan business portfolio. But duty out of respect and love and loyalty? Maybe not. He wanted what he wanted. He was an O'Sullivan. Arrogant.

Used to getting his own way. Her father had been telling her this for years. She should have listened. But suddenly none of that mattered now. She had one thought, one motivator… and that was protecting the child growing inside her. From everything and everyone. Including Liam. Her parents. And the whole damned world if necessary.

There was only one option. Only one way to make sure her baby wasn't placed in the middle of an emotional mine-field. She knew exactly what she needed to do.

Kayla drew in a long breath and met his gaze straight on. "Liam, I want a divorce."

Chapter Four

Liam stared at her, unable to believe what he'd just heard. She was breathing hard, as though every gulp of air was an effort.

"What?" he barked out.

She winced and stepped back. "It's the only solution here, you have to see that. We can't possibly stay married and have our baby stuck in the middle of—"

"Divorce?" he shot back, sharper this time, cutting her off as a kind of slowly gathering rage wound up his limbs and then surged through his blood and across his skin. *"Divorce?"*

She visibly shrank back, putting space between them, but then her chin came up defiantly. "Don't shout at me."

Liam took a breath. And then another. He didn't want to shout. Or lose his temper. But this was too much. "I apologize for raising my voice," he said stiffly. "But, Kayla, there's no way in hell that I am going to divorce you."

He watched her, looking so beautiful and yet so vulnerable that his hands itched with the need to pull her close, to hold her and tell her everything would work out—that her parents would understand and everyone would make peace. But he couldn't. Because he knew it would taste like a lie. Liam didn't have any idea if it would work out. He only knew that Kayla was his wife and she was having his baby. Nothing else mattered. Nothing else ever would.

"Then I'll divorce you," she said, her voice a little unsteady.

"On what grounds?" he asked and took a few steps toward her, grasping her hand. She looked up and met his gaze. Her fingers were warm and familiar and he linked them with his own. She didn't struggle. She didn't move. Her pupils were dark, searching his face, somehow drawing them closer together, almost as though she had some kind of magnetic tug on every part of him.

"I don't know…" she said, her voice faltering.

"Divorce isn't an option, Kayla," he said, squeezing her fingers just a little. "Not now. Not ever."

She shuddered. "But I don't know what else to do… I just…"

Moisture filled her eyes and even though she blinked quickly, tears brimmed and tipped down her face. Liam gently touched her cheek, wiping at the tears with his thumb. "It'll work out," he said quietly. "I promise."

She stilled, resistant and unsure. "I wish…I wish I had your faith in everything…and in them."

"Have faith in *us*," he said and drew her closer. "In this," he said and tenderly pressed a hand to her belly. Knowing their child lay beneath his palm, protected and growing inside the woman he loved, was like nothing he'd ever experienced before and emotion instantly clogged his throat. "Kayla…" He whispered her name, suddenly desperate to hold her, to kiss her, to make her see that they could get through anything as long as they stuck together. "We can do this."

She stared at him and then slowly, excruciatingly, shook her head. "I don't…I don't think we can." She pulled away and stepped back, folding her arms across her chest. "It's too hard. Too much. My parents…"

"You're putting your parents first in this?" he asked coolly. "Is that it?"

She shook her head. "I'm putting my baby first."

"*Our* baby," he reminded her.

She sighed heavily, as though she was suddenly all out of argument. "I'm tired, Liam. I'd like to go home and get my car so I can get back to work this afternoon."

Her words punctured his chest like a blade. "*This* is your home," he reminded her. "Remember?"

She flashed him a heated look. "You know what I mean. Would you take me back?"

"Of course," Liam replied, feeling the weight of her rejection sit so heavily on his shoulders that he had to step away and place a steadying hand on the countertop. "If that's what you really want."

"I don't know what I want," she admitted quietly. "Or how to feel. Or what to do. All I know is that everyone I love is going to be hurt in one way or another." She sighed heavily. "I'll just get my bag."

Liam watched as she headed from the room and was still standing by the counter when she returned a few minutes later. She *did* look tired. And like she wanted to be anywhere but where she was in that moment. He was suddenly torn between love and rage and knowing only Kayla had the power to make him feel that way. Liam swallowed back his burgeoning resentment, grabbed his keys and then shouldered into a jacket.

"Let's go."

She followed him wordlessly, not speaking until they were both outside and strapped into his Silverado.

"You're angry?" she said quietly, shuffling her bag on her knees.

He wasn't about to deny it. "Damned right."

"And I suppose you think I'm a scared little girl who's too afraid to confront her parents?" she inquired, her jaw tight. "Does that about cover it?"

"Bravo," he said and started the engine. "You have me all figured out."

She sucked in a long breath. "You can be such a jerk sometimes."

He knew that. But she was maddening. Infuriating. And he genuinely didn't want to see her upset. But she was being as inflexible as a rock. She stayed quiet on the trip back to her apartment and by the time Liam pulled up to the curb he was all out of patience. He killed the engine, unclipped his seat belt and turned to face her.

"I'm sorry for shouting before. But we need to talk about this, Kayla."

She shrugged one shoulder. "We've talked enough for one day. I'm exhausted. I'll talk to you soon."

"Soon?" he echoed, thinking she made talking to him sound like the thing she wanted to do least in the world. "And your parents?"

Her brows furrowed. "I'll tell them in the next couple of days."

Days? Liam didn't want it dragged out any longer than necessary. "I'd like to tell my parents, Kayla…sooner rather than later."

"I understand. And of course I can't stop you from telling your folks…but I would ask that you give me a couple of days to talk to my parents first."

He nodded fractionally. "Okay. How about we both do it by Friday? I have a meeting tomorrow with my father and your dad's lawyer," he said, watching as her frown increased. "It's about that commercial property down on Howard Street that they've jointly owned for over thirty years. It appears that your dad is finally prepared to sell his share in the place."

They both knew that the dispute over the large allotment had been going on for decades. After nearly two years, Liam had finally succeeded in getting Derek Rickard to negotiate…at a steep price and only through his lawyer—who was new to town and had been some New York high-flier until he'd recently married one of Kayla's friends. But Liam was confident he'd secure the property. His plan had been to tie up the loose ends around the Rickard family… which of course was moot now, considering Kayla was his wife and was having his baby.

"So, by Friday," she said quietly, nodding. "Sure. I'll call you when it's done."

And then…

It was the question burning on the edge of his tongue. Liam wasn't sure he was prepared for her to tell him she wasn't coming home. He clenched his hands as tightly as he could stand. "And will you come back home once you've told your parents?"

She stayed quiet for a moment, her hands clutched in her lap. "I'm not sure what I'll do," she said finally, and with such hollowness that his insides ached. "I learned a lot today, Liam," she said as she opened the door, but turned to look at him. "I learned that I'm pregnant, and realized that I will do whatever it takes to protect my baby. I also learned that you think you can snap your fingers and I'll simply comply with whatever demand you make. But I won't," she said quietly. Her tone was as damning as if she'd yelled at him in anger. "You are exactly what my father said you were—arrogant and entitled and so used to getting your own way that you don't care who you walk over. Well, you can't treat me that way…and I won't raise my child that way. So you've given me a lot to think about." She gazed out the window for a moment, then opened the door. "Goodbye, Liam… I'll talk to you soon. Thanks for the ride."

Liam sat wordlessly as she got out of the vehicle and closed the door. The ache in his chest grew as he watched her walk up the path and disappear inside the Victorian. *Arrogant. Entitled. I won't raise my child that way.* Her words stuck like a chant, replaying over and over. Was that really what she believed of him? That it was *all* he was? The notion hurt him deeper than anything else ever had before.

Then he shifted the gears and drove off.

Kayla wasn't sure how she would function at work after the day she'd had. It was half past one by the time she walked into the museum and dumped her bag in her office. Shirley was there to greet her, all smiles at the successful day and the large party of tourists that had been through the place that morning. The gift shop had been busy and the older woman quickly did an inventory of all the things that had sold. Kayla managed to get through the exchange with a smile and a few cursory nods before Shirley clocked out for the day and she was alone. Then Kayla made tea, found a quiet spot on a chaise in one corner of the museum and sat down.

With a heavy sigh she thought about her life, her baby, her parents…and her husband.

The look on Liam's face when she'd left him earlier spoke louder than words. Rage, disbelief, hurt…it was all there for her to see. And she had almost capitulated and fallen straight into his arms and said to hell with everything and everyone else. *Almost.* The part of her that was all about doing the right thing held her back. She wouldn't make any decisions until she'd told her parents about their relationship and the baby. And she wasn't going to be railroaded.

Kayla got to her feet, sighed and headed back to her office. She made a few telephone calls about the upcoming benefit regarding catering and then placed a call to her doctor's office, making an appointment for Friday at lunchtime. Three groups of visitors came through during the afternoon, and she was just closing up for the day with plans to spend an hour doing some much-needed admin work when her mother dropped by to see her. She flipped the outside shingle to say the place was closed and ushered her mother inside.

Marion Rickard was mother earth. After several failed pregnancies early in her marriage, she'd had Kayla when she was thirty-nine years old. Kayla knew her parents considered her something of a miracle child, and that was why they loved her so fiercely. Smothered her, she sometimes felt. But she adored her parents and was grateful for the unconditional love they had bestowed on her all her life. And she had always done her best to make them proud. She'd achieved high grades in school and then attended a good college. After college she worked at the museum in Denver and had a long-term relationship with a respectable professor, always knowing her parents were proud of her achievements. When she'd returned to Cedar River permanently it was exactly what they wanted. She knew they expected her to marry and start a family. And that was what Kayla wanted, too...except for one major complication...

Liam.

"Everything all right?" Her mother's voice jerked her back into the present as she prepared a pot of her mother's favored peppermint tea in the staff room. "You seem distracted."

"I'm fine," she fibbed and brought the pot and two small mugs to the table. "Just tired."

"You've been working long hours," her mother remarked as they sat down. "And you've probably been doing too much organizing for the benefit. Why it had to be held here at the museum, I don't know. There are plenty of—"

"I volunteered for it to be held here," Kayla explained. "And it's been a gratifying experience being on the hospital committee and helping with the event. The hospital needs this money that this benefit will bring, Mom. It's important to our town."

Her mother nodded. "I know, but I don't like to see you looking so pale and exhausted."

Kayla almost blurted out the reason why she looked like so tired. *Almost.* Although her mother was definitely going to take the news better than her father, she felt she had to tell them together. "I'm fine, Mom. Just tired and hungry."

"Don't neglect your health, that's all I'm saying."

"I won't," Kayla promised. "And I'll drop by for dinner on the weekend, okay?"

Her mother nodded. "I'll make your favorite pasta."

"Sure," she said and smiled, thinking she wanted nothing more than to go home, strip off her clothes and soak in a bath for half an hour. But since she only had a shower at her apartment, that idea was off the table. She had a lingering thought about the huge spa tub at Liam's place. It was decadent and luxurious and large enough for two— something they'd taken advantage of many times during the last five months. Well, certainly in the early months of their relationship when she hadn't had to think about their unexpected Vegas marriage or having a baby on the way.

Her hand automatically rested on her abdomen and she felt an instant connection to the child in her womb. It was unlike any feeling she'd experienced before and Kayla had no idea how to compartmentalize her emotions. All her life she'd responded a certain way—being the loyal daughter, the caring friend and, when in an intimate relationship, the obliging girlfriend. But knowing her baby was inside her, Kayla didn't feel loyal or obliging. She felt the need to protect her child with such fierceness, such soul-wrenching intensity, that nothing else mattered—not even the heavy heart she experienced when her mother left a few minutes later. She'd always been unfailingly devoted to her parents and hated deceiving them... until now. Once she'd been to the doctor and had a checkup, only *then* would she tell them about the baby and Liam.

By the time she headed back to her apartment it was close to five o'clock. And she groaned inwardly when she spotted Liam's hulking Silverado parked outside. Not because she didn't want to see him. She simply didn't want to rehash the same discussion they'd had that morning. However, she quickly noticed that his truck was empty and there was no sign of him on the front porch. She was fishing for the apartment key on her key ring when she heard voices coming from the backyard. Kayla walked around the house and discovered her elderly neighbor, Mary, standing by the old gazebo and pointing upward. Then she noticed Liam, dangling high in the air off a rickety old ladder, with Mary's old ginger cat tucked under one arm.

"Oh, yes," Mary said breathlessly. "That's good. He's safe now."

By the time Kayla reached the gazebo, Liam was halfway down the ladder, while a clearly distressed Mary had her arms outstretched, ready to retrieve her precious pet. Jinx was renowned around the Victorian for getting trapped on top of the old gazebo. Usually it was Dane or Mr. Cartwright from the ground-floor apartment who was wrangled into getting the cat down. But not today.

Liam noticed her the moment he stepped off the ladder and passed the feline to its owner. He smiled and her insides immediately did a silly flip. Even after everything they were going through, he could still make her weak at the knees. She looked him over, spotted his jacket and a brown grocery bag strewn across the grass. His hair was mussed and his shirt torn down one sleeve. Obviously Jinx hadn't wanted to come down from his comfy spot easily.

"Everything okay here?" Kayla asked and stood beside Mary.

Her neighbor gave a long and relieved sigh. "Oh, yes, thanks to this young man. My poor little Jinx got himself wedged up there and he couldn't get down," Mary said as she pressed the cat against her chest.

"You should take Jinx inside," Kayla suggested gently and smiled. "You know how he gets wanderlust in the evenings."

Mary nodded. "Yes. And the poor little dear can hardly see much these days. Thank you," she said, grinning broadly as she turned her attention back toward Liam and then tutted. "Oh, look at your shirt. I can try and repair it for you, if you want to take it off now I'll see that it's—"

"Ah, no," Liam said quickly, clearly not prepared to derobe in front of the older woman. "It's fine. I'm just glad that your pet is okay."

Mary smiled, blushed a little and then nodded, openly in the throes of a little hero worship. "Jinx is all I have," she said and turned, tearing up before saying one final thank-you to Liam and then muttering soothing words to her now purring cat as she headed back to the house.

Once the older woman was inside and out of sight, Kayla turned her attention back toward her husband. "Looks like you just made a friend for life," she said and smiled. "Although she did seem awfully keen to get you out of your clothes."

He grinned. "Jealous?"

Kayla laughed and the sound caught on the breeze. "I'm not the jealous type," she said as she stepped closer and saw that his shirt was torn in a few places. "And I don't think that shirt can be salvaged. Come upstairs and you can change into something else. I'm sure there are a couple of your shirts in my wardrobe."

"Sure." He nodded as he grabbed his jacket and the brown bag and then held out his closed fist, slowly opening his palm. "Although I don't think that's my biggest problem at the moment."

Kayla saw the blood congealed in the middle of his hand and rushed to his side, grabbing his fingers and holding his palm upward. "You're hurt? Why didn't you say so?" She examined the injury. "It looks deep. It might need stitches."

He shook his head. "It's not that bad. I must have caught a nail up there."

Kayla gave him a gentle shove in the direction of the house and entered through the back, keeping his injured hand suspended between them. Once they were upstairs in her apartment she sat him at the dining table and retrieved the first-aid kit from the bathroom. It took a few minutes to clean and swab the wound and then cover it with a plaster strip. It wasn't as deep as she'd first thought and didn't need stitches.

"That should do it," she said and stood. "I'll just go and grab you a shirt."

When she returned he was standing by the sofa, shirtless, and she sucked in a breath at the sight of him. His smooth, tanned skin had its usual effect on her and attraction, deep and heartfelt, surged through her. Her gaze moved over him slowly, across his broad shoulders, muscled arms and chest, and down to the six-pack that always had the power to make her weak at the knees. Never in her life had she ever found any man as attractive as she found Liam. It wasn't simply a reaction to his good looks. It went much deeper. It was alchemy, chemistry, a kind of soul-to-soul connection that had a will and power all of its own. And she knew he felt it, too. Knew he was as drawn to her as she was to him.

"You sure you want me to put that on?" he asked silkily, gesturing to the shirt she had in her hands.

Kayla swallowed hard and passed him the shirt. "Positive. Don't want you catching a chill."

His mouth twisted. "It's as warm as toast in here," he said as he pulled on the polo and flattened it over his stomach. "In case you hadn't noticed."

She *had* noticed. She was hot. All over. But not from the temperature in the room or the fact that it was mild and still sunny outside. But because the man in front of her was so damned gorgeous. Kayla shrugged lightly. "How's the hand?"

"Fine," he replied. "Thank you."

Kayla crossed her arms, ignoring the fluttering in her belly. "So, what are you doing here?"

He grinned, like he'd been expecting the question from the moment they'd clapped eyes on one another. "You mean besides untangling your neighbor's cat from the roof of that broken-down gazebo?"

"Yes," she replied. "Other than the heroics, why are you here?"

"I needed to see you," he said flatly. "Six hours ago you told me you wanted a divorce... I'm pretty sure we still need to talk about that."

Guilt pressed down on her shoulders. "It was an emotional moment...and I was...I was..."

"I know that," he said gently and she melted. Damn... sometimes Liam O'Sullivan could be the just about the sweetest man on the planet. "Which is why I'm here." He grabbed the small brown bag and held it up. "For you," he said and smiled. "I dropped by the Muffin Box and grabbed some of that fancy tea you like and a few of those salted caramel, dairy-free brownies."

Kayla's heart pounded. "Oh…that was very thoughtful. Thank you."

He shrugged and then his expression narrowed. "Have you eaten much today?"

She knew that look. Liam could be something of a worrier when it came to her diet, even though he was a strong-coffee, cold-pizza kind of guy. "I had breakfast and lunch," she said, thinking it was a stretch to call the three bites of a sandwich she'd had at midday any kind of adequate meal, but she wasn't about to embellish on the fact.

"You know you need to snack during the day," he said. "Did you make an appointment with your doctor?"

Kayla nodded, watching as he dropped the brown bag on the table behind the sofa, crossed his arms loosely and looked at her. Through her, she thought, searching her face with eyes so blue she didn't dare look away. There were questions in his gaze. And tenderness and anguish, too.

"You know," he said slowly, swallowing hard, "I don't mean to come across as demanding or *entitled*…or anything else you seem to think of me."

There was hurt in his words. Words that were an echo of what she'd said to him earlier that day. "I know you don't mean to."

"But it's in my blood, right?" he shot back. "In my DNA to be an arrogant jerk who thinks he can snap his fingers and have the world come running? Does that about cover it?"

Shame, sharp and abrasive, sliced between her shoulders blades. And something else, a niggling sense of resentment that had been building all day. Maybe longer. Since she'd first told him she thought she was pregnant. Since he'd shown up unannounced to her apartment the night before. Since he'd insisted they go to Rapid City together. And since he'd driven her back to his house so she could take the pregnancy test and then demanded she tell her family about the baby and their marriage. In the last twenty-four hours Kayla had discovered that she didn't like being told what to do. The resentment wavered for a second, allowing guilt to surge forward. Like a seesaw, she shifted from one emotion to the next, caught between loathing and loving him in that moment. Of course, loving him won out. Because she *was* in love with Liam, despite their complicated relationship.

"I guess we can't help who we are," she said quietly. "Including me. I know you think I'm a coward."

"Is that what I think?" he asked, his dark brows raised slightly.

Kayla shrugged. "You must. *I* do."

He took a few strides across the room until they were barely a foot apart. He grabbed her hand and raised it to his mouth, softly kissing her knuckles. "For the record, I don't think you're a coward, Kayla. But you're right about one thing, I am used to getting my own way. So, I'll spend the next two nights alone in *our* house, because I promised I'd give you the time you need to tell your folks. But once everyone knows, I want you back…permanently. This isn't a request," he continued when she pursed her lips in protest. "And you can call me arrogant and demanding and entitled and everything else you have in that arsenal of yours. But you're my wife and you're carrying my child—and I want you both back home by Friday night."

Then he kissed her. Hot and hard and with possession stamped all over it. When he released her she stepped back, breathing heavily, her lips tingling, her knees wobbling. She didn't have a chance to protest. Or to beg him to kiss her again. Because he grabbed his jacket and left the apartment without another word.

It took Kayla an hour before she managed to calm her nerves. She drank a cup of the tea he'd brought her and nibbled on the brownies. She tried to keep her thoughts occupied that evening with television and then a novel, but neither worked, so she had a shower and climbed into bed by eight thirty. By midnight Kayla was still staring at the ceiling and by the time she rolled out of bed the following morning she was tired, aching and tempted to call in sick for work. She didn't, and instead arrived at the museum just before nine o'clock.

"We have the bus tour from Rapid City arriving at ten," Shirley reminded her once she'd flipped the shingle to the open sign.

Kayla nodded wearily and did a swift visual inventory of the gallery before she spent some time with the older woman in the gift shop. They discussed the impending arrival of a new range of craft work from a local Lakota artist that was certain to sell quickly. By ten o'clock the tourists arrived and she spent half an hour giving a tour of the exhibits in the museum and art gallery. When she was done, Shirley took over the group and Kayla headed back to her office.

She was halfway there when she experienced a sudden lethargy in her limbs. Sweat broke out over her brows and she grabbed on to a chair by the gift shop to steady herself. Her fingers were suddenly numb and she swayed, losing hold of the chair. Somewhere, through the white noise now screeching between her ears, Kayla heard a concerned voice call her name. And as she fell to the floor she peered up and saw the blur of half a dozen faces staring down at her. There were more voices. More whispers. More white noise. And then when she finally closed her eyes, blackness wrapped around her as her hand instinctively lay on her belly, and then Kayla had only one coherent thought.

Liam...

Chapter Five

Spending time with his father was never really a chore. But Liam wasn't in any kind of mood to think about business or locking up a deal with Derek Rickard's hard-ass lawyer. Tyler Madden was good, he'd give him that. The deal to buy the warehouse was on paper and all they had to do was sign and then get Rickard to do the same. Easy. Only, his father was quibbling about three old trucks that had been left inside the building decades ago and apparently had some sentimental value to both men. But Liam didn't care. He wanted the papers signed, the meeting to be over, and then to get back to his office and suffer in silence.

"They are my trucks," he heard his father say and then Liam rolled his eyes. An easy contract negotiation this *wasn't* going to be. Not when two hardheads like his dad and Derek Rickard were involved. "If Rickard hasn't the backbone to be here for this meeting then he doesn't get to have everything his own way. Call him now and tell him I want what's mine or the deal is off."

Tyler nodded and jotted something down on the notepad in front of him and looked about as impatient with the negotiations as Liam felt. The other man put a call through, had a brief conversation and then ended the call, frowning as he returned his attention to them.

"From your expression I take it that didn't go so well?" Liam inquired cynically.

Tyler shook his head. "My client isn't in a position to make any changes to this agreement today," he said and filed the contract into a folder on his desk.

"And why the hell not?" Liam heard his father shoot back irritably.

"Something personal has come up. It seems his daughter has been taken to the hospital and he's not available to…"

Liam didn't hear anything else. He sprang to his feet as though his heels were on fire and was out the door so fast he barely heard his father calling his name as he raced through the office, past the secretary stationed in the reception area and then headed out to the street. By the time he reached his Silverado his hands were shaking so badly he could barely get the vehicle open.

The ten-minute drive to the community hospital seemed like the longest of his life and he pulled into the parking lot across two car spaces and didn't waste time changing the fact. Liam was through the doors to the ER within half a minute and standing agitated by the reception desk, demanding to see Kayla and the details of her condition. Of course the nurse behind the desk knew who he was. He was easily recognized around the town and had spent enough time on the hospital committee to be familiar to the staff.

The twentysomething nurse looked flustered. "Oh, Mr.

O'Sullivan, I can't give that information out to anyone but family and—"

"Liam?"

He stilled, faintly recognizing the voice saying his name. He turned and saw Lucy Monero moving toward him. Lucy was a doctor on staff in the ER and one of Kayla's closest friends.

He walked three steps to reach her. "Is she okay?" No introduction. No small talk. All he cared about was the condition of his wife and baby.

Lucy smiled gently and summoned him away from the reception desk. "We can talk over here," she said and made her way into a private corner of the foyer. He followed her instantly and endured another agonizing few seconds before she spoke again. "She's fine," Lucy said gently. "She passed out at work and was brought here as a precaution."

Passed out? Liam's gut churned. "Is the... Is she... Is everything..." His words trailed hopelessly.

"She's fine," Lucy assured him. "*Everything* is fine."

The way she said the words made him realize that Lucy knew about the baby. "She told you she's pregnant?"

"Yes," Lucy said and nodded.

"And the baby...the baby's okay?"

Lucy nodded again and smiled. "Perfectly fine. And Kayla's had something to eat and drink and her vitals are all normal. I think she fainted because she hasn't eaten much the last couple of days. She'll be able to go home this afternoon."

Relief flooded through him and then guilt reared its head. Damn. He should have made sure she was eating properly, given her condition. He'd been so busy giving her ultimatums he hadn't spared a thought to how she was *feeling*. He had some serious ground to make up.

"What can I do?"

"Make sure she eats regularly and healthily," Lucy said, suddenly all physician. "It's extra important considering her history of anemia. Particularly now she's pregnant. And no stress," she added and raised her brows.

Liam expelled a heavy breath. "That might not be so easy, considering the circumstances."

Lucy expression tightened. "She's my best friend, Liam. I love her dearly. But it's as her doctor that I'm saying this. She's under a lot of pressure and that's bad for her *and* the baby. She needs to relax and rest and eat and stop stressing, or this might happen again. And maybe she won't be at the museum the next time. Maybe she'll be driving her car or crossing the street. But you're a smart guy, so I'm sure you'll figure out a way to fix this."

His stomach churned again. "I'd like to see her."

"Sure," Lucy said and sighed. "Her parents are here, but I sent them to the cafeteria while I examined her. I'll keep them occupied for a while."

"Do they know?" he asked, stupidly feeling about eighteen years old.

Lucy patted his arm. "You'll have to ask Kayla that. She's in room 4B, just down the hall."

Liam waited only seconds before he strode through the foyer and down the hall. When he reached her room the door was open. She lay on the bed, on her side, her beautiful hair fanned out on the pillow. But she looked pale and there were dark circles beneath her eyes. She appeared to be sleeping, so he entered the room quietly and stood by the bed. But when her lids opened and he caught sight of her anguished and vulnerable expression, he caved and dropped to his haunches beside the bed, grasping her hand and holding it tightly within his own.

"Honey…" The word left his lips on an agonized groan. "I'm here."

She hiccupped and swallowed hard. "I'm so... I'm sorry... I was about to call you. I just closed my eyes for moment."

Liam noticed her cell phone on the bed. "Don't worry about that. I spoke to Lucy, she said you're going to be fine."

She nodded. "I know. I fainted at work. One moment I was standing, the next I was on the floor. Lucy said the baby was okay...but I was so worried."

"Me, too," he admitted, his voice raw, and pressed her knuckles to his lips. "But I'm here now. And you're fine and the baby is safe and everything will be okay."

She sighed, as though it was the hardest thing she'd done in an age. "I guess I should have eaten all those brownies," she said and her mouth creased into a tiny smile as she gestured to the tray of hospital food on the small table at the foot of the bed. "I just ate half a sandwich and a cup of Jell-O and I feel much better now."

Liam's insides contracted so much they hurt. "It looks as though I'm in charge of making sure you eat right from now on."

"Coffee and cold pizza?" She screwed up her nose. "Yuck."

"I'll make you some of that risotto you like...as long as you promise to take care of yourself, okay?"

She nodded and sat up a little. "I'm sorry that you were worried. How did you find out I was here?"

He briefly explained about the aborted meeting with her father's lawyer and then pulled a chair up beside the bed. He held her hand, linking their fingers together. The need to protect her and keep her safe surged through him with the power of a freight train. "Your folks are here. Did you tell them?"

She took a breath. "They're still down as my next of kin so the hospital called them. They don't know about the baby yet...they only know I fainted at work. Lucy made them leave so I could be examined." She shrugged and sighed. "But I'm pretty sure my dad is probably in the cafeteria having conniptions over the fact that I fainted. You know how protective he gets. Or rather, overprotective."

Liam didn't disagree. "If it's any consolation, my father probably thinks I've lost my mind the way I raced out of Tyler Madden's office earlier."

She laughed softly and the sound hit him directly in the solar plexus. "You should probably go," she said, suddenly serious again. "They'll be back soon and I think—"

"Not a chance," Liam said and kissed her hand again. "We do this together."

She opened her mouth to protest but then anything she was about to say was quickly moot. Because there was a shuffling noise by the doorway. And then a voice.

"What the hell is going on here?"

Liam was on his feet in a microsecond and swiveled on his heels. Derek Rickard stood in the doorway, red-faced, eyes ablaze and clearly unhappy about seeing his beloved daughter sharing space with the son of the man he hated most in the world. But Liam stayed where he was, holding Kayla's hand tightly, feeling her struggle through to his bones.

"Dad…"

Liam didn't miss the way her father's gaze latched onto the fact that he was still holding Kayla's hand and he glared at him. "Get out of here, O'Sullivan, before I—"

"Dad!" Kayla implored and she sat up farther. "Mom, please…let me explain. I need to tell you something important and please try to understand." He heard her draw in a long, almost agonized breath. "Liam and I are…we're… we're together."

Her mother gasped and there was a sudden and deafening silence in the room as Derek and Marion Rickard

crossed the threshold. Liam stood firm, unblinking, prepared to protect Kayla by whatever means were required.
Their gazes flicked from their daughter to Liam, and then
back again, clearly trying to work out what Kayla was saying. And when the penny dropped it was loud and shattering and filled with a kind of unholy disbelief.

"No…no…no…" Derek Rickard's voice trailed off for a
moment. "That's impossible. It can't be true."

"Dad," Kayla said quietly. "It is true. Liam and I are—"

"Are you actually telling me that you're with *him*?
O'Sullivan's son?"

"Yes," she whispered. "We've been together for five
months and—"

"What the hell is wrong with you?" her father demanded,
cutting her off.

Liam's spine straightened instantly. Enough was enough.
"Mr. Rickard," he said slowly, carefully, fighting the growing rage crawling over his skin. He felt Kayla's fingers
tighten beneath his, but he was too wound up to stay quiet
any longer. "With all due respect, you will not speak to my
wife in that way."

Liam wasn't sure he'd ever heard silence sound as loud.
But there was silence. A load of it. Silence and disbelief
and plain old hatred swirling in the air. And most of it directed at him.

Then Derek Rickard started shaking his head and his
eyes almost popped out. "Your *what*?"

"My wife," Liam said again, slowly, quietly and without
blinking. "And the mother of my child."

Marion gasped again, sharper this time, and the anger emanating from her father was so palpable, Liam instinctively
stepped closer to her, almost shielding her from their view.

Derek Rickard took a few steps into the room, glaring at

his daughter and shaking his head. "Child?" the other man echoed with clear disbelief. "You're pregnant? To him?"

"Kayla," Marion Rickard whispered hollowly, speaking for the first time since they'd entered the room. "How could you?"

Derek continued to shake his head in a blustering, undignified fashion. "I just don't believe it."

"It's all true, Dad," Kayla said, her voice calmer than he'd expected it to be. "I am pregnant. And Liam and I got married a month ago."

It was as bad as she'd expected. No…worse. Her parents were looking at her as though she'd committed the worst kind of sin, and Liam was standing as rigid as a statue beside her. She sat up and swung her legs off the bed, still a little dizzy, but this was a conversation she needed to have.

"You're going to be grandparents in about seven months' time."

Her father's eyes were filled with so much anger and pain that she actually felt it deep within her bones. But now it was done, and there was no way to avoid hurting her parents. And her main priority was staying calm and protecting her baby.

"I don't want to discuss this in front of *him*," her father said harshly, casting Liam a death stare.

Kayla knew she had no chance of getting Liam to leave. She also knew her father was stubborn and meant what he said. She looked toward her mother for support and saw so much hurt in her mother's expression that it made her ache inside. And she realized there was no coming back from this…no way to make amends. She'd done the one thing they would find unforgivable…she'd betrayed them by falling in love with Liam.

It was playing out exactly as she'd known it would.

And then her heart began to break.

"I'm sorry," she said, her voice wavering, and she felt Liam's grip on her hand tighten. "I'm so sorry…"

"Mr. and Mrs. Rickard," Liam said quietly, his voice strong and familiar and still not enough to stop her heart from shattering into tiny pieces. "I know this situation will be difficult for you to accept…but it isn't up for negotiation. We're not teenagers and don't need your permission to be together, although I know your blessing would mean the world to Kayla."

"I'll never give it," her father shot back. "You would be the last man on earth that I would want for my daughter."

She felt Liam flinch slightly, but he stayed resolute. "I'm sorry that you feel that way. But I am in love with Kayla."

"Love?" Her father's voice chilled her to the bone. "You people don't know the meaning of the word. Do you know what this is?" He shook his head and Kayla saw tears in her father's eyes. "This is history repeating itself."

And within seconds her father was gone from the room. Kayla looked toward her mother earnestly, looking for allegiance, forgiveness…or something that would let her know that the breach she'd created was reparable. "Mom… please…try and talk to him. Try and make him understand."

Her mother's expression softened. "I don't think that will ever happen. But I will try, for your dad's sake…and for yours."

A small surge of relief flowed through her. "Thank you, I know he'll listen to you. And Mom…what did he mean by history repeating itself? What history?"

"I can't talk about it… It's better left in the past. That's where it belongs." Her mother shook her head hopelessly. "You two have no idea what you've done."

"Mrs. Rickard," Liam said, gentler this time. "If there's

something we should know, it's better we find out now than later."

Kayla watched as her mother straightened her shoulders and drew in a long breath. "Be careful what you ask for, Liam...you might find you don't like the answer."

When her mother turned and left, Kayla slumped back. She wanted to cry, but was strangely out of tears. More than anything else, she wanted answers. She pulled her hand from Liam's and sat up straight in the bed.

"Do you have any idea what they were talking about?"

He shook his head. "Not a clue. You?"

"No. What my dad said about history repeating itself makes no sense. What history? When?"

He shrugged. "How about we talk about this later. You need to rest and—"

"Stop trying to pacify me, Liam. I'm rested and I ate something and I feel a lot better than I did a couple of hours ago. I was stupid to neglect my diet," she admitted. "And I won't be doing that again while I'm pregnant. But I want to know what my father was talking about. And I want to know why my mom thinks that *you* won't like what we find out. Don't you?"

"Of course," he replied. "But right now, I'm more concerned about you being rested and well enough to come home."

Home? There was no chance of that when everything was in such turmoil. "Once I'm out of here I need to go and see my parents."

He frowned. "Maybe you should leave it for a while. You know, give them some time to get used to the idea. How about we go and see them on the weekend?"

"No. I need to see them today."

"You're not being sensible, Kayla. For starters, you haven't even been released from hospital yet and—"

"I'll check myself out," she said defiantly.

"Oh, no, you won't. If Lucy gives you the all-clear, then I'll take you home." He clearly saw her frown so he back-pedaled a little. "I meant, to your apartment, since you prefer. But no more stress today, okay?"

"Then stop stressing me out by telling me what I can and can't do," she shot back. "You've been demanding I set everything straight for the past month, right? Well, that's what I want to do." Her expression softened a little. "And I'm sorry about what my father said...you know, about you being the last man on earth and all that. I'm sure he didn't mean it...not really."

Liam's mouth twitched. "Oh, I'm pretty sure he did. But it doesn't matter, Kayla. All that matters is what *you* think."

In that moment she didn't really want to *think* about anything other than getting the answers to the questions in her head. When Lucy returned a few minutes later Kayla requested she be released immediately, much to Liam's disapproval. But her friend examined her again and said she would be able to leave in a couple of hours. She ate some more food under her husband's watchful gaze and then insisted she needed to rest for an hour. Liam left, albeit begrudgingly, and said he had a few things to do at the office before he'd come back to collect her. Kayla was glad for the reprieve, and once he was gone, she rested for a while, before Lucy returned and she endured a round of questions from her friend.

"So, you guys are married?" Lucy asked, perched on the edge of the bed.

"Yep."

"Did you have any plans to let your best friend know?"

Kayla sighed heavily. "Of course. It's just really...complicated."

Lucy smiled and nodded. "I get that. You just married

the one man your father has categorically said was a no-go zone for years. Even when we were at school I can remember your dad saying to steer clear of the O'Sullivan boys. And Liam in particular since he's the most like his father. I mean, we all know what people say about them, that they're cold and arrogant and only think about money."

Kayla's shoulders twitched. "He's not like that at all."

"He's not?" Lucy's brows rose dramatically.

"No," she replied. "He's generous and caring and actually very…sweet."

"Sweet?"

Kayla sighed a little impatiently. "I'm not about to get into a debate about Liam's character. I'm sure he's as flawed as the rest of us."

"I didn't mean to upset you," Lucy said gently. "I'm worried, that's all. I just want you to be happy."

"I want that, too."

"And does Liam make you happy?"

She shrugged. "Liam makes me crazy. And annoyed. And outraged. And…breathless…and utterly weak at the knees."

Lucy smiled. "You really love him? That's…great."

"It's inconvenient," she said and tried to garner some humor in her expression. "Since I should probably divorce him and make things right with my parents."

Her friend's face screwed up instantly. "You're not, though, right? Going to divorce him, I mean?"

"I don't know what I'm going to do," she admitted and sighed heavily. "I married Liam on a foolish whim one insanely passionate weekend in Vegas. And I didn't take the time to consider the consequences. But today, right here in this room when I witnessed my father's broken heart… *that* is the consequence of my actions. And I don't know how I'm going to live with that."

Lucy squeezed her arm and Kayla gratefully accepted her friend's comforting hand.

"Are you ready to go?"

Liam's deep voice was suddenly all she heard. She snapped her head around and saw him standing in the doorway, his eyes so dark they were almost black. Lucy got to her feet and said she'd go and sign the release form. Once her friend was out of the room, Kayla slid out of bed.

"All set," she said and smiled fractionally.

He came farther into the room and held out her tote and a jacket. "When I left here earlier I stopped by the museum and collected these for you."

"That was very thoughtful."

He shrugged. "Shirley said she has the place covered for the rest of the day."

Kayla bit back a grin imagining Shirley getting all flustered dealing with Liam, who she once said was as handsome as the devil and probably just as unpredictable. "Thanks. I'll call her later." She noticed how tense his jaw was. "Everything okay?"

"Sure. Let's go."

He grasped her elbow and her skin instantly tingled from his touch. But she didn't pull away. She looked up, meeting his gaze. But there was a hardness to his expression that hadn't been there an hour ago. "What's wrong?"

"Nothing," he replied. "Let's go and see your parents."

Once she was released and said a final goodbye to Lucy, they walked out toward the hospital parking area. It was a warm afternoon, typical of a spring day, and Kayla relished the feel of the sunshine on her face. The drive to her parents' home was done in silence. She knew something was bugging him. When he had something on his mind Liam always turned quiet and brooding. They pulled up outside the big, double-story home, with its perfectly manicured gardens and white picket fence, and he killed the engine.

"Just so you know," he said quietly. "If your father can't keep his temper in check then I am getting you out of here. Don't ask me to stand by and allow him to insult you… because I won't."

She swallowed hard. "That was out of character for him," she said, remembering the things her father had said at the hospital. "He's usually very respectful of other people and—"

"I don't care about other people," he said, cutting her off. "I care that he doesn't insult *you*. And stop making excuses for his bad behavior. That's something of a habit of yours."

Kayla grabbed the door handle. "Are we going to have an argument right now? Because if so, I don't think I'm up for it."

He got out of the car and came around the passenger side as she was getting out. "No, we're not going to argue. We're on the same side," he said and closed the door. "Remember?"

By the time they walked up the path and reached the porch, Kayla was so wound up she could have turned on her heels and fled. But the door opened before they'd pressed a foot on the bottom step and her mother opened the front screen.

"Should you be out of the hospital?" she asked, her face looking older than Kayla had ever seen before.

"I'm fine, Mom," Kayla assured her. "I've eaten and feel perfectly normal. But we really need to talk some more." She shifted a little closer to Liam. "All of us."

Her mother nodded, almost as though she'd been expecting them. "Your father is upstairs resting," she said as they walked through the door and entered the hall. "I'll go and get him."

As her mother disappeared upstairs, Kayla walked through the hallway and into the front living area. The room was big, filled with polished furniture, two leather chaise lounges and a huge fireplace. There were dozens of photographs on the mantel, most of them of her as a child and teenager. Some were taken with her astride her pony, Tickles. And another taken on the day she'd gotten her license and her folks had bought her a car, complete with a pink bow on the hood. Above the fireplace was a family portrait from the day of her college graduation. Her parents stood by her side in the picture, clearly beaming with pride. To an outsider, it would probably look like two people who overloved, overprotected and overindulged their only child.

She turned and saw that Liam was still standing in the doorway, arms at his sides, watching her with a small smile that warmed her through to the roots of her hair. In dark trousers, an immaculate white shirt and maroon tie, he was too handsome for words. Kayla met his gaze and was consumed by a wave of feelings so intense she grabbed the mantel for support. He walked toward her slowly and met her by the fireplace.

"You okay?" he asked, concern in his tone.

Kayla nodded. "Just try not to antagonize my dad, okay?"

"I think my very presence will do that."

"You're right." Her father's voice cut through their conversation and she turned her gaze toward the doorway. Her parents stood together, a unified front. "And since this is the first time an O'Sullivan has been in my home for thirty years, I trust you'll both respect that this is difficult for my wife and I. Speaking of respect," her father went on to say, sounding more like a robot than the man she'd adored all her life. "Kayla, your mother pointed out that I was rude to you earlier...so, for that, I apologize."

Kayla noticed the way her mother's hand rested on her dad's shoulder. They were a tight unit. Utterly devoted and loyal to one another, her parents had a strong and enviable marriage, something she one day hoped to emulate.

"It's okay, Dad," she said and tried to muster a smile as they walked into the room. "I know it must have been a shock."

"Shock?" he echoed. "Yes, it certainly was." His gaze flicked toward Liam. "Is. So, does *your* family know?"

"No," Liam replied stiffly. "Kayla wanted to tell you both first."

Her father's mouth twisted. "I can't imagine your old man being any more pleased about this than I am."

"Probably not," Liam replied. "But, it's done."

"Nothing that can't be undone."

Kayla felt Liam turn rigid beside her and her hand immediately came out to rest on his arm. She felt the muscles bunch tightly beneath her palm and gripped him harder. "Dad, we didn't come here to discuss our relationship."

Her father's eyes widened. "Then why are you here? If it's for my approval, that's not going to happen."

Kayla took a steadying breath. "I want to know what you meant at the hospital."

He waved a dismissive hand. "No, you don't."

"I do," she implored. "You said something about history repeating itself... What does that mean? I get the sense it has something to do with this feud between you and Liam's father and I just—"

"Feud?" her father said, cutting her off. "It's not a feud. I hate the man," he said with so much vehemence that Kayla flinched. She glanced at Liam and saw he was standing rigidly still. "I hate J.D. O'Sullivan's lies and his deception and every despicable thing he stands for."

"What the hell does that mean?" Liam shot the words out like rapid gunfire.

"You'll have to ask him."

"I'm asking *you*," Liam demanded.

The tension in the room suddenly escalated and Kayla's grip on Liam increased tenfold. She glanced toward her mother and saw helplessness in the older woman's expression. Something felt very wrong...as though words were about to be said that would change lives forever.

"Ask *him*," her father hissed. "Ask J.D. O'Sullivan about the lie he's lived for the past three decades. Ask him about my sister. Ask him about Kathleen!"

Kayla gasped. Her aunt Kathleen? Her gaze drifted to an old picture on the mantel of a young woman with light blond hair and brown eyes. A woman she'd never met and who was rarely mentioned.

"Dad, what are you talking—"

"Ask him about the eighteen-year-old girl he seduced and then ran out of town," her father continued his rant, red-faced, clearly pushed to the edge. "And then ask him about the illegitimate son she bore him twenty-nine years ago!"

Chapter Six

Liam felt as though the room had suddenly tilted to some crazy, other-world angle. He tried to make sense of the words coming from Derek Rickard's mouth. And failed.

Kathleen? His father? An illegitimate son?

There was no sense to be made. None. Rickard was just stirring up trouble. Bad-mouthing his father for reasons of his own. And then rage gathered slowly in his gut, swirling up like a funnel, heating his blood with its intensity. He glanced toward Kayla and saw confusion and then panic in her eyes. He wanted to calm her, to make things right. But he couldn't muster the strength to do anything other than stare blankly at the man who'd made the terrible accusation.

He found his voice and hated that it sounded raspy and desperate. "What are you talking about?"

Derek's mouth thinned and he laughed humorlessly. "About my sister. And your father. About the whole tawdry and disgraceful situation."

"You're lying."

"Ask him yourself," the other man said. "Ask him how he had an affair with my sister, got her pregnant and then forced her to leave town because he knew the scandal would ruin him."

Liam's head throbbed. It couldn't be true. His father was a lot of things, but the idea he'd betrayed his mother and their family in such a way? It was incomprehensible. Out of the question.

But when he looked at Marion Rickard he saw no lie in her eyes, and in that moment the world shifted, mocking him and everything he believed he was. He thought about his family. He thought about his life. His past. His present. And knew that suddenly it had all changed. Kayla grasped his arm tighter, as though sensing his sudden dive into a place that was filled with despair and disbelief and a kind of mounting helplessness that rocked him to the very core of his soul.

"I have to get out of here," he said the words low in his throat, only for Kayla to hear them. "I have to talk to my father."

"I can't leave them now," she whispered. "I have to stay."

Her words were like puncture wounds. She was staying. She was choosing sides.

Resentment replaced his despair and settled in his belly. "Suit yourself," he said as he pulled away from her grasp and then walked across the room, desperate to keep moving.

When he reached the doorway Marion spoke to him. "I did warn you that you might not like what you find out, Liam."

Within seconds he was down the hall and out of the house. By the time he reached his vehicle his chest was pounding and he was forced to sit behind the wheel and suck in several long breaths to control his haywire breathing.

Get a grip...

He tried not to think of Kayla as he headed off. Tried not to remember she'd made it clear where she stood. Because it hurt so much he could barely breathe.

He rang his father's cell, but it went to voice mail. There was nothing unusual about that since his father hated cell phones. Then he called the hotel and was informed his father had turned up looking for him earlier than afternoon, but hadn't hung around.

It took fifteen minutes to drive to his parents' home, set on fifty acres of prime grazing land that hadn't seen a head of cattle for decades. The painted fences, long driveway and manicured lawns led to the sprawling white ranch house that was elegant enough to grace the cover of a magazine. Seven bedrooms, five bathrooms, three living areas, a game room, and indoor pool and spa...it was the perfect home, the grandest in the county. But although he'd been happy enough growing up among the luxury, Liam preferred his quiet house by the river.

He spotted his father's Range Rover in the driveway and the tightness in his chest increased. It was Thursday—he knew his mother played bridge on Thursdays. Which was just as well, since the conversation he intended having with his father wasn't one he wanted to share with his mom.

When Liam entered the house he found his father in the kitchen, rifling through the refrigerator. He was a big man, tall and broad-shouldered, and at sixty one, still fit and active. As a boy he'd idolized his dad. His father was a giant. A superhero. Infallible. Indestructible.

When he entered the room his father stopped what he was doing, looked at him and frowned.

"What happened to you today? I went to the hotel looking for you. You took off from that meeting without so much as a—"

Liam walked toward the dining table, rested both hands

on the back of one of the timber chairs and spoke. "I went to be with my wife."

His father fumbled with the bowl in his hand and closed the fridge. "What?"

"My wife," he said flatly. "I got married a month ago."

"Married?" J.D. said the word as though he'd misheard. "You got married? Who the hell to?"

"Kayla Rickard."

The moment he said her name his father's expression shifted from disbelief to shock. "Derek Rickard's daughter? The pretty blonde from the museum?"

Liam stiffened at his father's disregard. "You know exactly who she is."

"Sure I do," J.D. replied and shrugged. "She was at the hospital? That's why you left the meeting?"

"Correct."

"Is she okay?"

Liam nodded. "She's fine."

"So, you're married to Derek Rickard's daughter? Why the hell are you telling me this now and not four weeks ago? Why the secrecy?" His brows rose. "Did you knock her up?"

Anger weaved its way up his spine. Now was *not* the time to talk about the baby. He didn't want to share the news. Didn't want it tainted by the conversation. "We thought we'd wait a while to tell everyone, considering how certain people would react to the news. But you know how the truth is, *Dad*...eventually it always comes out."

The pulse in his father's cheek beat erratically and he realized the other man looked uncharacteristically cornered. "Is there some point you're trying to make, Liam?"

"Yes," he replied tightly. "I want you to tell me the truth. I want you to tell me about Kathleen."

"What?"

"You heard me. Kathleen… Derek Rickard's sister. Tell me what she is to you?"

Liam watched as his father moved to the counter and set the bowl down. "I don't want to—"

"Tell me what she is to you!" Liam demanded and slammed a fist on the table.

His father stilled and sucked in a breath. Silence stretched for an age. Like elastic. Creating distance and then drawing them back together. The truth teetered on the edge of the air, until finally, his father spoke quietly. "She's the mother of my son."

Liam's chest tightened inexplicably. His father had another son. *A child with another woman.* Pain seared through his blood when he thought of his own mother. Of Kieran and Sean and Liz and his nieces. Of his family. Of what it would mean when it was revealed. And then of Marion Rickard's words: *Be careful what you ask for, Liam…you might find you don't like the answer.*

He drew in a long and steady breath. "Does Mom know?"

J.D. shook his head. "No."

It was betrayal of the worst possible kind. Lies and decades of deception. It was as though everything he'd known was suddenly a facade. "You cheating bastard."

His father winced. "You don't understand what I—"

"I understand enough. I understand that you got Derek Rickard's teenage sister pregnant while you were married to *my* mother and have lied about it for thirty years." Bile rose in his throat as he said the words and he swallowed hard.

"I had to," his father said quietly. "I had a family I had to protect… I had responsibilities and—"

"You had a responsibility to be loyal to your wife," Liam shot back. "But I guess loyalty and honor aren't that important to you, are they, *Dad*?" In that moment he almost hated saying the word. "But secrecy obviously is."

J.D.'s mouth twisted. "You're right, I'm a cheating bastard," he admitted and shrugged. "I had an affair and betrayed my wife. I'm guilty as charged. But it looks like you've kept your own secrets, too."

Liam laughed humorlessly. "Kayla and I kept our relationship under wraps because Derek Rickard hates you and by extension he hates me and everyone named O'Sullivan. I didn't know why up until half an hour ago. But now I do. Now I understand."

His father stepped around the counter. "Are you going to tell your mother?"

"No," Liam said flatly. "You are. And you're going to tell her today."

Then he spun on his heels and strode from the room.

He knew his father would follow him. J.D. O'Sullivan wasn't a man who took kindly to ultimatums. By the time he was out the front door and on the porch his father was a few steps behind him.

"Liam, you don't realize what you're saying," his dad said, breathing hard. "It's better this way. Better for everyone. Better for you and your brothers. Better for your mother. And better for Kathleen and Jonah and I won't be—"

"Jonah?" The word left his mouth like poison. "He has a name?"

"Well, of course he has a name. He's my son and I—"

Liam laughed painfully, cutting off his father. "My God, of course… You still see them."

J.D. didn't deny it. "I see Jonah occasionally."

"And he knows about us? About Mom and your life in Cedar River?"

"He knows."

Liam's chest tightened. "And what about Kathleen? Is that what this is? Do you have some kind of two-family thing going on, *Dad*?" Liam was so wound up, so mad with his father in that moment that he could have hiked up the three steps and punched him in the face. "Oregon," he said caustically. "That's where they are, right? Those fishing trips you sometimes take with your old *college buddies*? Those trips that Kieran and I begged to go on so many times when we were kids, but were told were always off-limits… That's where you went. To another state to be with your *other* family?"

"It wasn't like that," his father said, coming down the steps. "I went to see Jonah, not Kathleen. Once she left town we didn't have that kind of relationship. I promise you."

I promise you…

They were hollow words. Like the ones he and Kayla had made to one another a month earlier. *Love, honor, cherish.* Empty. Meaningless.

Liam stepped back and shook his head. "The thing is, Dad, your promises don't mean a damn thing anymore."

Then he got into his truck and drove off.

By the time she spotted Liam's pickup barreling down the driveway it was close to six o'clock. Kayla had been sitting on the veranda for half an hour, upset, but determined to keep herself together. Things had gone from bad to worse at her parents'. Her mother had tried to pacify her father, but he wasn't having any of it, and in the end, Kayla had given up, telling her mother she'd call the following day. It left her with a heavy heart. All her life she'd tried to do the right thing, to make her parents proud. And the one time she'd followed her heart, all she'd done was hurt the two people who had loved her most in the world.

Kayla watched as Liam pulled up outside the house and

got out of the truck. He looked beat. Worn out. And more alone that she'd thought possible.

He looked surprised to see her and stalled by the bottom step. "I didn't expect to see you here," he said, always straight to the point. "Are you all right?"

She shrugged. "Sort of. You?"

He took a second. "Since my life kind of imploded today, I've been better."

Kayla's heart ached and she got to her feet. "I'm so sorry, Liam… I had no idea."

He took the steps slowly and when he reached her Kayla walked directly to him. He seemed remote…as impenetrable as a marble statue. Until she pressed closer, wrapped her arms around his waist and held on to him tightly. She heard him sigh, felt his body loosen against hers, almost against his own will. A few seconds later she felt his breath in her hair, his hands on her shoulders and then down her back, until they rested on her hips. It was so good to be close to him, to inhale the subtle woodsy male scent of his cologne and feel his chest rise and fall with each breath he took.

"How are you really feeling?" he asked and pulled apart a fraction so he could reach her chin and tilt her face toward his. "No lingering effects from this morning? No more fainting?"

"I'm fine," she assured him. "I've had another snack this afternoon so I'm back to normal. And I bought the fixings to make spaghetti," she said and gestured to the shopping bag by the door.

"You're staying for dinner?"

"If that's okay?"

His grasp on her chin tightened a little. "This is your home. It's *our* home."

He kissed her gently, covering her mouth with his in a way that was both familiar and new. Kayla pressed against him and he deepened the kiss, drawing her tongue into his mouth, instantly hitching up the heat between them. She sighed and gave herself up to the moment, holding on as he anchored her head with one hand and kissed her like nothing else and no one else existed.

"God, I've missed you," he said raggedly against her mouth and then trailed his lips to her jaw and the delicate skin below her ear. "I've missed this."

Kayla knew the tension between them over the past few days had been partly fuelled by a complete lack of intimacy. She hadn't spent a night at the house in over a week and it had been days before that since they'd made love. At the beginning of their relationship, in those first couple of idyllic months where they'd been wrapped in a kind of hazy couple bubble, they used to make love every day. Liam hadn't been able to get enough of her and she had relished in the mind-blowing sexual chemistry they shared. And then, something had changed. Even before their impromptu wedding…Kayla had felt herself pulling away. As the sex and desire turned into something more, into a deep kind of love, she had begun to slowly close down. Because in her heart, she knew they were heading toward the impossible. She began spending more and more time at her apartment, using work and the upcoming benefit as a reason to put distance and build a wall between them, until there was very little left of their relationship that resembled those first weeks they'd been together.

"I've missed you, too," she admitted and inhaled the scent of him.

Liam tensed, almost as though the words caused him pain. "Let's go inside."

He released her, stepped aside to grab the grocery bag and opened the front door. Peanuts came meowing the moment they crossed the threshold and Kayla stooped down to pet the cat before she headed to the kitchen. Liam was behind her in seconds and dumped the bag on the counter.

There was suddenly a restlessness in the air between them. Kayla watched him, his shoulders tight, his impassive features giving nothing away. "What happened with your father?"

He shrugged. "He didn't deny it."

"Did you expect him to?"

"I'm not sure what I expected," he replied.

Kayla rested against the countertop. "My dad said that it had been going on for a few months before he found out. He and your father were friends…best friends. This is what came between them. Kathleen was my dad's little sister. Your father was thirty-one at the time, and my aunt eighteen. Did you know that she was your babysitter?"

"I remember," he said quietly.

Kayla nodded. "You would have been about five and Kieran three-and-a-half. My mother said Liz was still a baby and your mom was probably pregnant with Sean… you know…when it all happened."

"It kinda all adds to the whole sordid story, doesn't it?"

She felt his pain through to the roots of her hair. "I'm so sorry Liam… I can't imagine how hard this must be for you. And I can't fathom how difficult it's going to be trying to keep this from getting out."

He stilled and stared at her. "Getting out?"

"Your mom," she said quickly. "She doesn't know. She never knew about the affair. That's why Kathleen left town. That's why she had her baby in secret and why it's been kept that way for thirty years…to protect your mom and four innocent children." Kayla saw Liam's hard expression and knew he wasn't convinced. "Everyone believed my father and yours had fallen out over a business deal gone bad. No one knew the truth and my parents promised your father they wouldn't say anything."

"It didn't stop them from letting it all out of the bag today, though, did it?"

She nodded and touched her belly. "I think finding out about us being married and the baby and everything, it just spilled out. Let's face it, things were pretty heated between you and my dad for a few minutes and it was as though something had to give. I'm sure they felt bad once you left, especially my mom. And I tried to talk with them after you'd gone. Even though my dad shut down and would hardly speak to me. That's why I stayed this afternoon—I wanted to find out what really happened."

"I thought you stayed because you were choosing sides."

"Sides?" she echoed.

"Sure," he replied. "Your family on one side, mine on the other. Let's face it, Kayla, your father is never going to accept us being together. He made that very clear today."

"He was angry."

"I know," he shot back. "And he has every right considering what happened with his sister and my dad. But right now he's not the issue. *We* are."

"I don't understand what you—"

"We're *married*," he said with emphasis.

And he was angry. Furious. With her and probably at the world in that moment.

"I know that."

He expelled a heavy breath. "If you know that, why didn't you leave with me this afternoon?"

Shame clicked at her heels. He was right. Part of her knew that. But her divided loyalties made making that choice impossible. "They needed me to—"

"*I* needed you," he fired back. "Which means you have to make a decision… Be daddy's little girl, or be my wife."

She tried to ignore both the insult and the ultimatum in his words. And failed. "I'm here," she said and gestured to the house around them. "Aren't I?"

"I don't know," he said flatly. "Are you? And are you here for just tonight? Or maybe two? You know, I'm not exactly sure what being married should feel like, but I'm pretty sure this isn't it." He made a scoffing sound. "I suppose that's what you get when you marry someone on a foolish whim one insanely passionate weekend in Vegas."

Kayla's feet were suddenly entrenched in cement and regret licked over her skin. "You heard me say that to Lucy this morning?"

"I did."

Guilt pressed between her shoulders. "I shouldn't have said it. I shouldn't have made light of our marriage. It was insensitive and stupid and—"

"And a bit like saying you wanted a divorce, right?"

She groaned. "Okay, you're right. All I've done for the past twenty-four hours is make one thoughtless remark after another. I just don't know what to do and—"

"This is what you do!" he shot back. "You act like a grown-up, like someone in charge of her own life—and not like a spoiled child afraid of her parents' disapproval." His cheeks were suddenly slashed with color. "But I guess when you've spent your life doing exactly what you're told, having an authentic thought of your own is pretty much impossible."

Kayla stepped back. It was out. Just what he thought. For months the words had been unsaid between them. Liam had been tiptoeing around his feelings and she had clamped her hands over her ears, unwilling to hear anything that resembled criticism. The news of J.D. O'Sullivan's infidelity and the secret of Kathleen's child had somehow become a catalyst—a symbol of everything that was wrong in their relationship.

"I can't take sides," she admitted, aching inside. "You know I can't knowingly hurt people."

"No?" His brows came up.

"You don't count," she said and then quickly realized how bad it sounded and backtracked immediately. "I mean, of course you *count*... I only mean—"

"I know exactly what you mean, Kayla," he said, so softly that it was worse than if he'd lost his temper. "You and your parents are this tight little unit and nothing gets in between that. But you're forgetting one thing," he continued, his eyes dark and glitteringly intense. "You're carrying *my* baby and I won't allow you to put a wall up between me and my child. Not ever. You think you know me, right? Let's see how well you know me if you try and stop me from seeing my son or daughter."

He sounded cold, ruthless...nothing like the man she'd grown to love over the past five months. But she also knew he was hurting and didn't need her histrionics, regardless of how tempted she was to tell him to go to the devil for being such an arrogant ass. He'd just discovered that his father had cheated on his mother *and* that he had a near thirty-year-old half brother. It wasn't rocket science to figure he wanted to lash out at whoever was in the firing line.

"I would never try to keep you from your child, Liam."

"Not even if it means defying your father's wishes?"

She sucked in a sharp breath. "I'm not a puppet, Liam. Nor am I as weak-willed as you seem to think. I'll do what's best for our child. *Our* child," she repeated with emphasis. "And maybe you won't always agree with my choices...and that's okay...because I don't always agree with you, either."

His mouth twisted and he sucked in a long breath. "Okay... I guess that's settled."

She nodded. "I'm going to make dinner," she said quietly and moved around the countertop. "Why don't you take a shower and try to relax."

"I'm relaxed enough."

She grinned a little. "Sure you are."

"I don't need to relax," he said irritably. "What I need is…is… I need…" He stopped speaking and looked at her. "I don't know what the hell I need. Maybe a do-over of today for starters." He ran a frustrated hand through his hair. "Anyway, you're the one who should be relaxing… Doctor's orders, remember?"

"I feel fine," she assured him. "Perfectly healthy."

He didn't exactly look convinced, but he nodded. "I think I will hit the shower."

Kayla watched him leave, heard him take the stairs and a few minutes later registered the faint hiss of the upstairs shower.

She began preparing dinner and was dicing tomatoes for the sauce when there was a knock on the door. Kayla wiped her hands and headed down the hallway. The sun had just set and as she opened the door she blinked a few times to adjust her sight to the sensor light now illuminating the porch.

Gwen O'Sullivan stood on the other side of the screen.

Tall, blue-eyed and still strikingly attractive, Liam's mother was a kind and generous woman—Kayla knew that firsthand from how much time and money she'd donated to both the hospital and the museum over the years. She had a warm spirit and was highly respected in town.

She took a deep breath, steeled herself for an inevitable inquisition and unlocked the screen door. "Hello, Mrs. O'Sullivan."

"Kayla," the older woman said and crossed the threshold. "I heard you were taken to the hospital this morning? I trust you're recovered now?"

"Fully," Kayla replied. "I fainted, but I feel fine now. I've been a little too busy to focus on eating right the past few days."

"I'm pleased to hear you're feeling better." She paused, the awkward moment hanging between them. "I'd like to speak with Liam if he's here."

"He is. He's in the shower," she explained and then colored hotly, feeling foolish and self-conscious at the implied intimacy in her words. "He shouldn't be too long."

By the time they stepped into the living area Kayla could feel heat rising up her neck at the other woman's close scrutiny. Gwen moved across the room and stood by the huge fireplace. The silence was uncomfortable, and she was about to break the ice by mentioning the weather when Liam's mother spoke.

"So, is it true that you're married to my son?"

"Yes."

"Do your parents know?"

"They do."

"I imagine they're not thrilled by the idea?"

"Not especially," Kayla replied. "But I'm sure they'll come around."

"I hope they do," Gwen said and sighed, dropping her gaze to Kayla's abdomen for a moment. "And are you pregnant?" she asked bluntly. "I only ask because my husband said something to Liam today and my son didn't deny it. J.D. assumed that your pregnancy is the reason you married."

She shook her head. "It's not. We only found out about the baby—"

"Yesterday." Liam's deep voice cut through her explanation and she turned on her heels. He came through the doorway, dressed in faded jeans and a black T-shirt. With his feet bare, his hair damp and his jaw cleanly shaven, he looked utterly masculine and sexy. "Hello, Mom. It's good to see you."

Gwen came across the room and gave him a swift but affectionate hug and then resumed her place by the hearth. "I won't deny that I was surprised when your father told me about your marriage." Her brows came up in a way that immediately reminded Kayla of Liam. "Considering our conversation at the hotel the other day. You remember the one?" she queried, brows still arched. "Where I said it was time you got married and settled down and you muttered something about having no time or inclination...or something like that."

Liam shrugged. "We had our reasons for keeping quiet."

"No doubt...but deception has never been your strong suit, Liam. It's one of things I admire most about you. Even as a child you always told the absolute truth."

"It was my doing, Mrs. O'Sullivan," Kayla said quickly. "I insisted we wait."

"You should probably call me Gwen," the older woman said. "Considering you're now my daughter-in-law. I suppose this came about because you've been spending so much time together working on the benefit and the plans to extend the museum?"

"Something like that," he replied flatly. "So, you spoke to Dad?" Liam asked, flipping the subject.

"Yes," Gwen replied. "And although neither of us approve of the cloak-and-dagger way you went about everything, it's done now and we all need to make the best of it. Especially since there is a child involved. Children are precious and should be protected...no matter what."

As the other woman spoke, Kayla instantly understood her parents' motives for maintaining such secrecy around her aunt's affair with Liam's father. Gwen O'Sullivan was a good person, sincere and compassionate, and she clearly adored her son. Thirty years ago Kayla's parents had agreed to keep J.D.'s infidelity a secret to ensure the O'Sullivan children were raised in a secure and loving home. Some things, she suspected, were best kept unsaid.

"Mom," Liam's voice refocused her attention. "What else did Dad tell you?"

"Else?" she echoed. "Only that you rushed out of your meeting this morning with Derek's lawyer and went to the hospital, and that you came to the house this afternoon and said you were married to Kayla."

"And that's all?"

"Yes. Why?"

Kayla saw Liam's shoulders twitch. His expression was blank. His eyes as dark as she'd ever seen them. The tension emanating from him was palpable and she instinctively knew what was about to happen.

And she also knew she had to do something about it. Before it was too late.

Chapter Seven

"I think I need to sit down... I feel woozy."

Liam's attention immediately shifted to his wife. Kayla wobbled and went to grab the back of the sofa, but he reached her within a microsecond.

"Steady," he said gently and grabbed her shoulders. "I've got you."

She sagged against him. "Oh...thank you."

His mother came forward and patted Kayla's arm. "You look tired, dear. I should go and let you get some rest. But you should both come out to the house on the weekend." She smiled gently. "I'm sure, in time, your father will come around, Liam. And hopefully so will your parents, Kayla."

Liam ensured Kayla was settled on the sofa and then walked his mother to the door. Guilt, raw and intense, wrapped around him and he had to stop the truth from pouring out. But with his wife feeling unwell, now wasn't the time to lay the whole sordid situation at his mother's feet. He watched her drive off and then returned to the living room, finding Kayla standing by the fireplace.

"You should be resting."

"I'm fine. I was faking it," she said bluntly.

"What? Why?"

"To stop you from doing something foolish."

Annoyance slid up his spine. "You had no right to—"

"Telling your mom won't change anything. It will only relieve your conscience for a moment. But I guarantee it will hurt her terribly, *and* you, once you see how much pain it causes her."

"She deserves to know the truth."

"Perhaps," she replied, her chin tilted at a determined angle. "But it's not your truth to tell, Liam. It's your dad's. When you get past being angry at your father, you'll realize that."

"This isn't about my father."

"No," she said, hands on hips, looking completely at ease. "This is about you and how you see everything in black or white. But life isn't like that. Life is sometimes gray. And messy. And complicated. Because people and feelings are messy and complicated."

"The truth isn't gray," he shot back. "The truth is simply the truth."

She took a long breath, shook her head a little and then smiled. "I get it, you know. Truth and honor…that's how you live your life. You always tell the truth, and sometimes that's construed as arrogance and a certain kind of coldness. And then there's honor," she said, relentless. "You expect the same in others and that makes you seem impatient and judgmental. But not everyone is stamped with that same code, Liam."

He shook his head. "You make me sound like some kind of narrow-minded despot."

"Of course you're not," she said and moved a few steps toward him. "But I know you were drafted into your job at the hotel without any real choice. I know that as the eldest son you were expected to take over the reins from your father and probably raise a son of your own to do the same one day. And I know that neither of your brothers had that same pressure put on them to stay in Cedar River and carry on the family name."

Her words sounded like a mix of insult and pity. "So, I'm the eldest of my siblings and I have responsibilities. Your point?"

"Control," she said quietly. "Absolute truth," she said, echoing his mother's words, "means absolute control. Over everything."

It was a direct hit. It wasn't the first time she'd accused him of being a control freak. "Are you serious? I've felt nothing but out of control since the moment you crashed into my car in the hotel parking lot."

"Exactly my point," she said, hands now on hips. "Isn't that why you've been insisting I tell my parents about us for the past five months? So you can get back that control. And now, suddenly, everything is so out of control all you can think to do is try to tie it up in some neat little package you want to stamp as the truth."

The message behind her words niggled at him down deep, but he dismissed it, relying on what he knew was right, was resolute. "My mother deserves to know he cheated on her."

"Then allow your father to tell her."

"I gave him that chance this afternoon. He didn't do it. He spoke to my mom…he had his window of opportunity."

"Maybe he's trying to find the courage."

"He's not a coward," Liam said harshly. "He just doesn't want to be caught in the biggest lie of his life. He had his chance to tell her today and he blew it."

She shook her head. "Dishing out ultimatums isn't the answer. And maybe he finds it hard living up to the standards of someone whose principles are set so rigidly above his own."

Liam stared at her, saw the determined tilt of her chin, the way her hands were splayed on her hips and the query in her eyes. She was challenging his core beliefs...that the truth mattered above all else. Which was why he'd struggled with his promise to her to keep their relationship a secret for so many months. It was a lie and went against everything he believed in. All his life he'd lived to a strict moral compass. *Don't lie. Don't cheat. And a man is only as good as his word.* It was who he was. Who he'd always aspired to be. Listening to Kayla's criticism made him realize how wide the divide was between their most basic values.

"I can't change who I am."

"Not even for the people you love, Liam?" she queried and walked across the room, stopping when she stood barely two feet from him. "I've always believed that we should do whatever we need to do for the people who are important to us...even if that means doing nothing at all."

Conflicted, Liam watched as she walked from the room, and realized that the divide between their values was also a rift that could pull their relationship apart. Maybe permanently.

Dinner was strained. But Kayla wasn't going to back down. She believed he was wrong and had no intention of being compliant. So, they ate mostly in silence. And while she tried to make conversation, he was quiet and brooding and clearly in a bad mood.

After dinner he offered to wash up and she didn't protest. She headed upstairs to shower and when she returned half an hour later dressed in jeans and a soft green sweater, she found Liam on the couch, a laptop on his knees, clicking keys and deep in thought.

"What are you doing?" she asked and sat beside him.

"Finding my secret half brother."

She gasped. "Really?"

He nodded and turned the laptop around. "Check it out for yourself."

Kayla stared at the screen and the newspaper article. There was a grainy picture of an incredibly good-looking man with dark brown hair and blue eyes. She read the article briefly. Jonah Rickard. Twenty-nine. Architect. A native of Portland. It went on to detail the illustrious award he'd been honored with as an achiever in his field.

"He looks…" Her words trailed off for a moment. "Like you. And Sean."

She saw Liam scowl and then shrug. "If you say so."

"He didn't take your father's name," she said, thinking about how the man in the picture was also her cousin. It was complicated stuff. "I wonder what he's like."

"I'm not sure I want to know."

"He's your brother."

"Half brother," Liam corrected. "And since he's known about us all his life, he's clearly not interested, either."

"It must have been difficult for him. I mean, knowing he had this extended family and not being able to make a connection without stirring up a whole lot of hurt for so many people."

"Maybe," Liam acquiesced and shrugged and placed the laptop on the coffee table. He shifted in his seat and grabbed her hand, entwining their fingers so intimately she was quickly short of breath. "So, are you staying tonight?"

"If that's what you want."

"I'm more interested in what *you* want," he said.

The thing was, Kayla didn't know quite what she wanted.

They could go upstairs and make love. It would be easy to fall into his arms and forget the turmoil of the day. There would be heat and pleasure and raw, explosive passion. "Okay, let's go to bed."

He didn't move, didn't do anything other than stroke her hand gently with his thumb. It was hypnotic and sexy and immediately hitched her libido up a few notches. Kayla saw his eyes darken and the tension emanating from him was palpable. There was desire in his gaze...and something else...something that was suddenly unfathomable.

"What?" she asked softly.

"Exactly," he said. "What's going on in that beautiful head of yours?"

"I thought—"

"That making love would fix things?" he asked, cutting her off.

"You said you wanted a do-over," she reminded him. "So I thought we could—"

"Use sex to block out everything else?" he asked, cutting her off again as he dropped her hand and abruptly got to his feet. "Like the fact that we have a fundamental difference of opinion about my mother and rest of my family knowing the truth?"

Kayla stood and watched, helpless as he walked toward the windows, arms crossed, clearly experiencing a kind of ethical crisis. She longed to help him, but in her heart she knew there was nothing she could do to make him realize that sometimes the fallout from the truth wasn't worth standing on such inflexible, moral high ground.

"I'm going to bed," she said quietly and then added, "if you want to join me."

But he didn't.

He slept on the couch or in one of the spare rooms downstairs. By the time she awoke the following morning around seven thirty, weary from staring at the ceiling most of the night, Kayla found a mug on the kitchen counter with a tea bag in it, and a note saying he'd left early for work and would call her later.

She made the tea, ate some cereal and fruit, dressed in black trousers and a white shirt and was parking her car outside the museum at eight thirty. Since she'd forgotten to pack her lunch for the day, Kayla walked half a block to the Muffin Box. It was a popular café and she stood in a line five deep before it was her turn for service.

"Kayla," said Vera Mathieson, the fiftysomething proprietor of the Muffin Box, when she reached the counter. "Low fat, decaf, soy latte and a savory muffin?"

Kayla grimaced inwardly, pondering when she'd become so predictable. "Great, thank you."

Vera nodded and smiled, then snatched a brief glance toward Kayla's left hand. "So...no wedding band?"

She stilled. "Sorry?"

"It's just that I heard about...you know...your recent marriage."

Recent marriage? Wedding band? Kayla felt as though she'd visibly paled. "I don't know how—"

"Dorothy Atkins mentioned something," Vera supplied.

Dorothy was her parents' neighbor and her mom's closest friend. And Vera's sister-in-law. Obviously her mother had shared some details. And news, it seems, had certainly traveled fast. "Oh, I see. Well, we're—"

"You're married?"

Another voice, from behind this time. Kayla turned her head and saw an old school friend, Annie Jamison, staring at her, eyes bulging, mouth agape.

"Married to who?" someone else asked.

"Liam O'Sullivan," Vera supplied in a kind of blood-curdling whisper that silenced the café for all of five seconds. Then, the entire place erupted in a crazy mishmash of chatter that had her head reeling. Questions were fired in her direction and before she had a chance to reply, Vera began happily telling the other patrons about the Vegas wedding and her trip to the hospital the day before. When someone used the word *pregnant*, she bailed, grabbing her latte and muffin, paying the cashier before she slipped out of the café as discreetly as she could.

By the time she opened the museum door she was out of breath and her knees were knocking. Right…so the whole town knew she was married to Liam and pregnant with his baby? Well, there was certainly no point in denying it. Which was exactly what she was faced with when Ash and Brooke came to visit her at nine thirty. She was puttering around in the gift shop, waiting for Shirley to arrive for her shift at eleven, when her friends came through the door.

"Pregnant?" Ash asked, dropping into a viewing chair. "And married?"

Brooke rested an elbow against the gift shop countertop. "To Liam? Um…did you marry him because you are pregnant?"

"No," she replied.

"Then you're…"

"In love with him? Yes," she said and took a breath, experiencing a heady kind of relief in finally being able to admit the truth to her friends. "I'm in love with Liam."

"Really?" Ash said, frowning. "I mean, I like Liam, but he's so…so…well, of course he's rich and good-looking and successful, but he's—"

"Kind, considerate, generous," she said, cutting her friend off. "And really sweet."

Okay, so maybe *sweet* was a stretch. But she wasn't about to stand by and allow him to be berated, not even by two of the people she cared about most.

Brooke smiled. "I don't think any of us saw *this* coming. I mean, I think we all knew you guys were in some kind of relationship…but marriage and a baby…wow," she said. "And Tyler said he took off from their meeting yesterday like a man possessed."

She explained about passing out at work and the brief hospital stint. "And I feel fine now," she added when she spotted their combined concern.

"And you're living with him?" Brooke, the more practical of the two, asked.

Her mouth twisted. "Well, that's where it gets complicated. At the moment I'm sharing time between my apartment and his house by the river."

"But if you're married and you're in love with him," Brooke said, frowning a little, "shouldn't you be living together full-time?"

Yes. But she didn't say it. The way they'd ended the evening together the night before wasn't exactly a postcard for a normal marriage. "The situation with my parents makes it hard to—"

"If they love you," Ash said quietly, interrupting her, "they'll understand."

Kayla stared at her friend. Ash knew about difficult parental relationships. She lived with her twice-divorced mother and had had a child when she was barely nineteen, fathered by a man who'd run out on her a few years later. As her friend, Kayla knew the story, and it was complicated stuff.

"I think they need some time to adjust," she said, deciding not to say anything about her aunt or Liam's half brother. "I'm sure it will work out," she said, not really believing her own words since her father's silence and her mom's tears the previous afternoon spoke volumes.

Her friends both nodded supportively and Kayla quickly switched the conversation to something less personal, which was the upcoming benefit. The event was only two weeks away, and Kayla still had to finalize the catering and the guest artists that were attending. It was black tie, with canapés and drinks, followed by a presentation of local artists and then an opportunity for patrons to bid on the art pieces that were being showcased and donated for the event. She was sure it would be a success, and since Liam was essentially funding the evening, she knew they needed to talk about some last-minute details.

Once her friends left, Kayla put in a call to Connie and asked to make an appointment to see him sometime that day.

"Ah...you want an appointment?" his assistant said. "You can see Liam anytime you like."

Kayla wasn't convinced. His curt note that morning wasn't exactly reassuring. "Around one o'clock, if possible," she said, remembering her doctor's appointment at midday. She ended the call and was busy with a few tourists looking through the museum for the next hour. When Shirley arrived, Kayla headed to her office and called her mother. It went directly to voice mail and she ended the call with a heavy heart. Building the bridge with her parents was not going to be easy. She was at her desk, sipping tea and finishing the last of her muffin when she heard a deep voice say her name. She looked up and spotted Liam standing in the doorway, arms crossed, one shoulder resting against the jamb. Her insides fluttered at how ridiculously handsome he looked in his suit. The red tie, knotted perfectly at his throat, the immaculate white shirt and charcoal jacket, which fitted him like a glove, amplified her attraction to him.

"I believe you wanted to see me?"

Kayla pushed her chair back and stood. "Yes. I need to go over a few things about the benefit. I thought I might speak to—"

"You know," he said and pushed himself off the frame, "you don't need to make an appointment. If you need me, I'll be here. Always."

Her knees wobbled. "Your note this morning was cryptic."

"No, it wasn't," he said quietly and walked toward her desk. "You were asleep and I didn't want to disturb you. I said I'd call you this morning, which I was about to do when you called Connie. Who, incidentally, seems to think we're in the middle of some sort of major crisis and probably would have told me off for being a jackass if I'd given her the opportunity."

"She's a smart woman."

He shrugged fractionally. "I think the crisis is happening in spite of us."

"You slept on the couch last night," she reminded him.

Color slashed his cheekbones. "I had some demons to work out."

"Really? And here I was thinking that the couch was my punishment for daring to disagree with you."

His mouth twisted. "Am I that much of a controlling jerk?"

She shrugged. "Sometimes. Goes with the territory of being in charge of everything and everyone, I suppose."

His eyes darkened. "Well, if it's any consolation, I'm pretty sure the punishment was all mine last night."

Kayla fought the urge to head straight for his arms. Instead, she concentrated on business. "I need to go over a few things about the benefit. It looks as though three of the four invited artists are going to be—"

"My mother has invited us to the ranch for lunch tomorrow," Liam said, cutting her off as he came around the desk. "Are you up for it?"

Kayla stilled. "I'm not sure...your father—"

"I'll keep him under control," Liam said and half smiled. "Okay?"

She nodded and fiddled with a few documents on her desk. "Sure. I've always liked your mom. But I would think it's more about how *you* feel about it, considering how things are between you and your dad."

He shrugged indifferently, but Kayla wasn't fooled. He was clearly tense and probably still angry about the way they'd left things the night before. But he was somewhat back in control of his feelings and it made her resentful. Stupid, of course. But there was no logic around loving someone. It got mashed in between feelings like lust, rage, impatience and judgment. And since Liam judged pretty much *everyone*, she experienced an inexplicable need to hang on to her resentment just a little longer.

"So, about the benefit," she said, all business. "Most of the RSVPs are back and I should have a final head count by next Wednesday. I'm meeting with Abby on Monday at three o'clock to go over the final catering requirements, and Connie and Ash said they'd help set up the seating and tables on Friday."

He was directly in front of her desk now, staring at her with blistering intensity. "Finished?"

Kayla frowned. "This benefit won't get organized by itself. I'm just trying to—"

"Avoid the difficult conversation?"

"Which is?"

"Are you coming home permanently?"

Kayla remembered Brooke's and Ash's disapproval about her indecisive living arrangements and tried to shrug off the question. "Well, I—"

"Because if you are, we can go to the apartment now, tell the geek upstairs that you're leaving and collect the rest of your things."

There it was—Liam being a bossy, controlling jerk! "Why? Because now the whole world knows about us there's no reason I shouldn't? And when I say the whole world, I mean that pretty much the entire town is gossiping about us. There was a fascinating conversation going on at the Muffin Box this morning about our marriage and the baby."

He shrugged one shoulder. "Gossip is inevitable."

"It doesn't bother you?"

"The truth doesn't bother me."

Right…the truth. His superpower. "I'll start packing up my things tomorrow," she said as a compromise. "And I won't lift anything heavy," she promised when she saw his frown. "I want to drop by and see my parents this evening, so I'll probably stay at my apartment." She checked her watch. "And now I have a doctor's appointment, so I should get going."

"We'll go together," he said easily, grabbing her bag before she could protest. "And since you made an appointment to see me at one o'clock, how about we head to JoJo's for lunch instead?"

JoJo's Pizza Parlor was one of Kayla's favorite haunts and he knew it. "Sure. But you don't need to come with me to the doctor. It's only a checkup and—"

"Together," he said, firmer this time. "You were admitted to the hospital yesterday… I'd like some assurance that you and the baby are okay."

"Fine," she said and took her bag. "I'll let Shirley know I'm heading out for a couple of hours."

A few minutes later she met him by the front door. Her doctor's office was a block down Main Street so they walked over, and when they were on the sidewalk Kayla almost jumped out of her skin when he grabbed her hand. She could feel that he was wearing his wedding band and a familiar surge of guilt wound its way through her blood. Two women who worked at one of the beauty parlors in town passed them and didn't bother to hide their surprise. Liam was high profile in the community and because of her job at the museum Kayla was well-known. The fact that they were walking the street together, holding hands, was sure to keep local tongues wagging for a day or so.

"Everything all right?" he asked as they walked.

"Fine," she replied and was pleased they quickly escaped into the doctor's office a few minutes later. Until the receptionist actually gasped when they arrived together.

"Relax," Liam said as they sat in the waiting area.

"People are staring," she whispered, leaning close. "And did you see the look on—"

"You really do worry way too much about what people think." A tiny smile tugged at his mouth. "Not ashamed of me, are you?"

Kayla's gaze narrowed. "Don't be an idiot. You're… you're…"

"Actually," he said quietly, "I think we've already established what you think of me. Controlling. Despotic. Irrationally honest."

"And a pain in the neck at times," she added and smiled sweetly.

Before he could respond they were ushered into the doctor's office. She endured Liam's scrutiny while Doctor Potts, a man who'd been her family's practitioner since before she was born, checked her blood pressure and got her to head off to the bathroom to do another pregnancy test. When the result came back positive, he withdrew some blood for further testing. They chatted about her diet and a prenatal program of exercise and vitamins and then he was summarily questioned by Liam about everything from traveling to sleep to having sex while pregnant.

"Did you have to ask that?" she said, still embarrassed and hot all over by the time they left the office and hit the pavement.

He shrugged. "I wanted some medical answers. Potts is your doctor. Why the sour face?"

"Because," she said, deliberately folding her arms across her chest so he couldn't grasp her hand. "I didn't go there for a sex talk."

He laughed. "Oh, honey, you do know that sex is the reason you're pregnant, right?"

"Very funny," she huffed. "And don't call me *honey*."

Liam's arm came around her shoulder and he drew her closer. "Get used to it. Now, I promised you a lunch date."

"Right now I'd rather chew glass than go to lunch with you."

He laughed again, seemingly oblivious to her bad mood. "One vegetarian JoJo's pizza coming up. And then I'll—"

He stopped abruptly when his father unexpectedly came through the door of the Muffin Box as they were walking by. Kayla stopped moving and felt Liam's grip on her shoulder tighten. J.D. O'Sullivan had a paper carry bag in his hands. He looked flustered, out of sorts, not his usual blustering, confident self.

"Liam… I was…I was just…" His words trailed off and he shook the small bag. "Peppermint brownies," he said and shrugged. "Your mother's favorite."

Liam looked unimpressed. "I suppose I'll see you tomorrow," he said and swiftly led Kayla away.

When they reached JoJo's he opened the door and ushered her inside. The place was busy, but the owner, Nicola Radici, was a mutual friend *and* an old flame of Liam's brother, Kieran, so they were quickly seated in a booth near the back.

"Are you ever going to forgive your dad?" she asked

bluntly, once Nicola was out of range. "Because it looked like all you wanted to do was punch him in the nose."

Liam met her gaze. "Firstly, I would never hit my father. And second, I'll work on my relationship with him once he tells my mother the truth."

"And if he doesn't?" she prompted. "Are you going to tell her?"

"Let's hope it doesn't come to that. Now, why don't we order?"

They ordered, ate and made a stilted effort at small talk for an hour. It was nearly two o'clock by the time they were back in her office. Kayla dropped her bag and rounded out her shoulders, aware that Liam watched her every move.

"I should get back to work. Shirley needs a break and I—"

She didn't get a chance to finish because he reached her in a couple of strides and hauled her into his arms, kissing her with a kind of possession that was so gloriously intense it weakened her knees. Kayla's hands instinctively moved up his shoulders and she kissed him back. His tongue found hers, drawing their mouths together with erotic intimacy. She sighed low in her throat, reeling in the sensation his kiss evoked and held on, gripping his shoulders, pressing closer until there wasn't space between them. When he pulled back she was breathless and panting and his hands lingered on her waist as he looked down into her upturned face.

"You're my wife," he said softly. "Remember that with all the craziness that is going on with our families."

He left abruptly and Kayla's lips were tingling long after he'd gone. She did some admin work for a while and later that afternoon called her mother again. She was surprised when her father answered the phone. She wanted to visit that evening, to try and heal the hurt that was growing between them, but her father insisted her mother had a headache. So, she hung up, telling her dad that she'd call the following day, before saying she loved him. Normally, he would say it back. But nothing was normal.

Kayla closed up the museum at five and headed back to her apartment. By six she was going through her wardrobe and packing a considerable portion of her clothes in two suitcases. By seven, she had written a list of things she needed to pack up the kitchen, including boxes, tissue and tape. And by eight she was showered, dressed in comfy sweats and sitting cross-legged on the sofa, watching television. Liam called at nine fifteen to bid her goodnight and by then she was so emotionally tangled that she let out a fractured sob and he only took about five seconds to respond.

"I'll be there in twenty minutes," he said and promptly hung up.

It took fifteen and when he tapped on the door she let him in and fell straight into his arms and cried. Deep, racking sobs that hurt her chest and burnt her throat.

"I feel so guilty. I've hurt them so much," she said and wept.

"Kayla…sweetheart…I promise you it will be okay."

Liam gathered her up and carried her to the bedroom, laying her down gently. He stretched out beside her, tilting her chin until she met his gaze. The dimness of the lamplit room created a cocoon-like feeling and she swallowed hard, unable to stop the flow of tears.

"You can't control how they feel, Kayla," he said gently. "As much as you want to. As much as it hurts. They have to get through this in their own time. But they'll come around. They love you."

She wanted to believe it. But it still hurt. Exhausted, Kayla pressed her face into his chest, feeling the steady beat of his heart against her cheek, and allowed herself to sleep. When she awoke the next morning it was past seven and she was alone. She could smell coffee and wrinkled her nose, pushing herself off the bed. She got to her feet and stretched, then took a quick shower, changed into a pale green dress and lightweight cream sweater and headed for the kitchen.

Liam was propped on a bench at the counter, sipping coffee. He looked up when she entered the room and smiled. "Good morning."

"Hi," she replied and grabbed a mug to make tea. "Um… thanks for coming around last night. I was pretty overwrought."

"That's my job, right?" he quipped. "I mean, looking after you. Do you feel better this morning?"

"Much," she replied, stretching the truth a little. "And you're right, I need to give my folks some space to adjust. So, what time are we going to see your parents?"

"I thought we'd leave around eleven," he replied. "Is there anything you'd like to do beforehand?"

She shrugged lightly. "Not especially. Shirley is working for a few hours this morning so I have the day off."

He nodded. "I see you packed a few things yesterday… We could take your stuff home if you like?"

"Sure," she said agreeably and then explained how she needed cartons and packing tape to finish the job. "And I need to give notice to Dane. I still have four months left on my lease so I'll have to find someone to sublet or—"

"Don't worry about that," Liam said, cutting her off as he slipped off the stool. "I'll pay the lease out and he can put the place up for rent again."

It was a generous gesture. "Okay."

His brows came up. "What? No argument?"

She shook her head. "I'm all out of arguments."

"Shall I go and tell him right now?" Liam inquired.

Kayla bit back a grin. "You know, you have no reason to be jealous of Dane."

He scowled. "It's a guy thing."

"It's a Liam O'Sullivan thing," she said and smiled extra sweetly. "Anyway, I'm pretty sure you make him nervous."

"Good."

She laughed. "You're such an alpha male of the species, Liam."

"For better or worse," he reminded her. "Remember?"

They spent a few hours moving her suitcases and some smaller items to his house and then headed to his parents' ranch by eleven. She'd never set foot inside the sprawling ranch house before and was awed by the sheer luxury of the place. The polished timber floors, raked ceilings, fittings and furniture were faultlessly put together and looked as stylish as a magazine spread. Liam took her hand, leading her through the house and out to the pool area out back.

Gwen O'Sullivan sat in a chair beneath a Balinese canopy. Dressed in white linen, she looked as stylish as her surroundings. She was drinking iced tea and staring out toward the huge pool. Liam greeted his mother with a perfunctory kiss on the cheek and squeezed her shoulder.

"Where's Dad?" he asked, looking around. "I didn't see his car out front."

Gwen turned in her seat and removed her sunglasses. Her red-rimmed eyes were unmissable. "He's gone."

Kayla gasped and she saw Liam's entire body turn to stone. "Gone?"

"Yes," she said, steadier now. "Gone. I kicked him out last night. I kicked every inch of that lying, cheating, no-good-son-of-a-bitch's ass to the curb. And it felt damned good."

Chapter Eight

A couple of things struck Liam simultaneously. First, his dad had told her the truth and now his parents' marriage was obviously in trouble. And second, his always refined and poised mother was using words like *ass* and *son of a bitch*. Something she'd never done before.

"You kicked him out?" He moved around the table and dropped into a chair. "Really?"

"Really," she confirmed.

Liam grasped his mother's hand and squeezed. "So, he told you?"

"About Kathleen? Yes."

"And…anything else?" he prompted.

"You mean the son he has with her?" She nodded unsteadily. "Yes…he told me everything. He told me about the affair. About the child. About the thirty-year-old secret he's been keeping. He almost seemed relieved once I knew. And a little surprised when I told him to leave," she added and shrugged. "But he left without making a scene. He probably stayed at the hotel last night."

Liam's insides churned. He'd expected arguments. Maybe hysterics. But he hadn't anticipated his mother would demand that his father leave the ranch they'd lived on together for thirty-five years.

"Mom, are you sure this is what you want? I know he made a—"

"I needed some time to think," she said and waved a hand. "And to admit to myself that our marriage has been in trouble for a long time."

Whoa. Not what he had expected to hear. His parents' marriage had always seemed…solid. Even through the difficult times, like his sister's death, they had stayed strong. Sure, they were very different people, but no two people in any relationship were without fundamental differences.

Liam glanced toward Kayla. She stood a few feet away, arms crossed, her expression one of sadness and concern.

"I want you to know, I don't blame your aunt," his mother said, looking directly toward Kayla. "I knew Kathleen… She was a sweet girl. I'd like to say she was some kind of temptress, but that's not who she was. I always believed the resentment between my husband and your father was fueled by a business deal gone bad… It never occurred to me that Kathleen had anything to do with it. But I understand now. The scandal would have been worse than the hatred between two men who had once been the closest of friends. And I was so busy back then I didn't take much notice of what was happening in my marriage. Maybe I didn't want to see. I had three young children and another on the way and I was doing a lot of community work. And J.D…." His mother sighed as her words trailed off for a moment. "J.D. said he fell in love with her. Even if I'd known,

I'm not sure there would have been anything I could have done to change what happened."

His father had loved Kathleen? Liam's mind reeled. And his mother, who he suspected was hurting through to her bones, was the picture of calmness and dignity. The need to fix her pain chugged through him like a freight train. But he knew there was little he could do, few words he could offer that would give her comfort. When his cell rang he was almost glad for the interruption. It was his brother, Kieran, and he answered the call quickly, excusing himself and heading inside so he could talk to his younger brother in private. He stood by the kitchen window, his gaze directed toward the pool area.

"What the hell is going on there?" his brother demanded before he could speak. "Dad just called. He said he's been kicked out of the house. I've been calling Mom all morning but it's been going straight to voice mail."

"I'm at the ranch right now," Liam said, then took a breath and quietly told his brother everything he knew. With half his attention focused on Kieran, the other half was on Kayla, who was now sitting beside his mother and holding her hand. It seemed an almost poignant picture. The two women he cared for most in the world, who had suddenly been brought together through chaos, were offering comfort to one another.

"So, we have a brother in Portland?" Kieran asked incredulously and spoke again before Liam could reply. "And you're married to Kayla Rickard and having a baby? Well, damn. Looks like I better get my tail back home, pronto, to help you deal with all of this."

"I can handle it."

Kieran sighed. "You're a hothead, just like Dad. So is Sean. I'm the only one with a lick of sense. I'll take some leave from the hospital and be there in a few days. Try not to make things worse until I get there."

Liam ignored his brother's sarcasm and ended the call. By the time he'd walked back outside his mother and Kayla were still deep in conversation. Their voices echoed and he caught their chatter about baby things and how much his mom liked being a grandmother. He stayed back, lingering by the gate, suddenly uneasy about interrupting them.

"I'm always up for babysitting," his mother said and smiled. "I so enjoy it when Grady brings the girls over for a visit. Not as often as I would like, mind you, but he's a good father to my granddaughters. And now we have another baby coming," she said and patted Kayla's arm. "That makes me happy. I know things seem difficult with your parents, Kayla, but just give them some time to get used to the news and soon they'll realize what a lovely blessing this is."

"I hope so," Kayla said quietly.

He was about to take a few steps closer when his mother spoke again.

"I can see that my son loves you very much. I hope that you care for him as much in return. Because he's going to need you. Liam has always had strong opinions about what's right and wrong. As a little boy he would get indignant and worked up about injustice or unfairness, even on the playground." She smiled and sighed. "My sons are all so different. Sean was always the troublemaker, Kieran was the peacemaker and Liam was the defender of principles. Which is why, despite how angry he is with J.D. at the moment, I know that he's going to find it the hardest to understand why I'm divorcing his father."

"Really? You've decided?"

"I made my decision this morning. I haven't been truly happy for a long time. This situation has made me reevaluate things. So, I'll talk to J.D. first and then tell my sons."

Polarized, Liam remained where he was for a moment and absorbed his mother's words. Had he imagined that divorce was the inevitable outcome of his father's betrayal? Had he believed his mother would end things? *No.* He definitely hadn't been prepared for the fallout from the truth he so righteously believed was his father's responsibility to tell.

He turned, headed back inside and called his youngest brother. Of course, the call went to voice mail. With the one-hour time difference, it was ten thirty in Los Angeles, and on a Saturday morning Sean was likely to still be in bed, hungover and wrapped around a leggy starlet or two. He left a brief message and ended the call.

Kayla and his mother walked inside soon after and he forced himself to stay cheerful as they chatted while preparing lunch. The conversation switched to the upcoming benefit and the hotel and despite the turmoil, there was almost a relaxed feeling in the room. Once they'd eaten, Kayla retreated to one of the bathrooms to freshen up and Liam was alone with his mother.

"Thanks, Mom," he said.

"For what?" she asked, frowning a little.

"For accepting Kayla amid this whole situation."

"I like Kayla," she replied and shut the dishwasher door. "I always have. And now she's your wife and I respect that. That's what families do...they respect one another's decisions."

For a moment he thought she was going to broach the subject of divorcing his father, but she didn't. So he changed tack. "I don't think Kayla's folks feel the same way."

"It's different for them," his mother said evenly. "They have one daughter, who they had after many years of trying to have a child. It's natural that they are protective of her."

"Overprotective," he muttered.

"Don't be too quick to judge them," she said and smiled. "You're going to be a father yourself in the not-too-distant future. And once that baby is put in your arms, anything else you've ever experienced will seem insignificant. Then you'll understand what it is to love this tiny, helpless and wonderful human being that you helped create."

Liam's throat felt inexplicably tight and he swallowed hard. His mother's strength had a life force of its own and he managed a wry smile. "Are you getting sentimental about being a grandmother again?"

"Probably. When you lose a child, priorities shift," she said quietly. "When your sister died, for a long time I never thought I would smile again, laugh again. But I did. My granddaughters helped heal the terrible loss I felt. And you helped. And Kieran and even Sean in his own way," she said and grinned. "What I'm trying to say is that Kayla's parents are just reacting to the hurt they feel. They're angry at your father and by association they're angry at you, too. Try and see this from their point of view. And Kayla's."

He did. And logically, he understood Derek and Marion Rickard's resentment. But logic wasn't going to help fix the problem. "It still needs to be made right."

"Sometimes, there is no right to be made. People are people, Liam. We mess things up. We overreact. Or we don't react at all."

"Mom, I heard you—"

His cell pealed and he saw his father's number on the screen. He ignored the call and pushed the phone back into his pocket. Kayla returned before he had a chance to say anything more and she looked so weary he figured he needed to take her home. They said goodbye to his mother and headed off a few minutes later.

"Everything all right?" she asked once they were pulling out of the driveway.

He nodded. "You look tired."

"I am," she admitted. "Maybe it's the baby hormones catching up with me."

"Home, then?"

"Yes. Home."

They didn't talk on the trip home and he remained silent when she excused herself and headed upstairs to rest. At a loose end and tired of being in his own head, Liam changed into a pair of old jeans and a blue T-shirt and took off for the boathouse. He hadn't spent any time lately working on the old, twenty-foot wooden vessel he'd been restoring for the last couple of years. It had belonged to his grandfather, and for Liam the restoration was a labor of love. Even though most of the interior was done, it was still a long way off getting back into the water, but he usually enjoyed the solitude and time-out. Kieran thought he was nuts for attempting the rebuild, but Liam liked the challenge and wasn't put off by the time it would take.

He flicked on some music, grabbed the tools he needed and got to work. A couple of hours had passed when he realized he wasn't alone. Kayla stood in the doorway, holding a couple of sodas. Liam jumped down from the stern, where he'd been sanding a length of new timber, and met her by the door.

She looked effortlessly pretty in a pale yellow sundress, silver sandals and her hair flowing around her shoulders. She passed him a soda and he flipped off the top. "Thanks," he said and took a long drink.

She stepped into the boathouse and ran a hand along the edge of the boat. "It's looking good. Your mom told me you've had the dream of getting this back onto the water for a long time."

He shrugged. "A fool's dream, maybe."

"You're no fool, Liam."

Just a fool for love...

All he wanted to do was haul her into his arms and lose himself in her touch. He was tired of thinking. Tired of feuding. Tired of every damned thing that was making him feel so wretchedly unhappy. She was back with her suitcases. Her clothes were hanging in the closet upstairs. But the distance between them still felt like an almost insurmountable divide. Her parents were barely communicating with her. His parents' marriage had imploded. Kieran was on his way back to Cedar River to save the day and Sean was probably still sleeping with every woman he met.

God, what a mess.

"I had a nice talk with your mom," she said and smiled. "About the baby."

"That's not all she said, was it?"

Kayla's expression narrowed. "I don't know—"

"I heard her tell you that she's divorcing my father."

"She was upset after finding out about Kathleen and Jonah."

"Not surprisingly. Anyway, it's not like I can do anything about it." He sighed heavily. "Looks like I'm a control freak without any control."

Her brows rose. "Are you looking for sympathy?"

"No. Kind of ironic, though, don't you think?"

Her shoulders lifted. "I'm glad it was your father who told your mom about everything."

"Saving me from myself and my rigid principles, you mean?"

"That's one way of putting it. Do you really think she'll divorce him?"

"My mother has a strong will," he replied and ran a hand down the edge of the boat. "But my father likes getting his own way. Whatever the outcome, I'm sure it's going to be messy."

"He loved her," she said and looked pained all of a sudden. "Your dad *loved* Kathleen. I wonder if he still does."

"He shuffled her off to Oregon, had a secret son with her and then lied his ass off to his family for years...that's not love."

"You mom said he was adamant that the relationship ended when Kathleen left town, but he has kept in contact with her because of his son." She sighed heavily. "You can't blame him for wanting to have a relationship with Jonah."

Liam scowled. "Can you stop saying his name like it should mean something to me. Because it doesn't."

"Sulking about it isn't going to make the fact that you have another brother disappear."

"Sulking?"

Her mouth twisted. "Isn't that why you're down here hammering away at this old boat?"

Annoyance crept through his blood. "I am not sulking. I was giving you some space." *I was putting space between us.* Damn, he hated it when she was right. Her brows were back up in that infuriating way and he ignored how it made his skin twitch. "Are you feeling better?"

"Yes. I had a solid gold nap and now I feel great."

Liam drank the rest of the soda and placed the bottle on a bench. "You look beautiful."

Her cheeks tinged with color. "You look hot."

"Thanks."

"I mean, working hard kind of hot," she qualified and then stammered a little. "Well, of course you're *hot*...argh... you know what I mean."

Liam laughed again and took the unopened bottle from her hands, laying it aside and then drawing her closer. "Can we stop talking for a while?"

"Did you have something else in mind?"

"Yes," he said, twisting her hair through his fingers and

anchoring her head gently. "I'd like to make out with my wife."

"And ruin a perfectly good argument?"

"To hell with arguments. To hell with everything and everybody. For the moment, at least." His throat felt tight and he met her gaze. "You're in my arms, but you feel so far away."

Her eyes shimmered, undoing him. "I'm right here," she whispered.

Liam sucked in a sharp breath. "Are you?"

She nodded. "Right here," she said again and her lips parted. "So, about this making-out thing?"

"I think that can be arranged."

Then he kissed her. Long and deep and with blistering intensity. Her hands came to his shoulders and she clung to him, urging him closer. Her mouth tasted sweet, like mint and green apple, and he plunged deeper, coaxing her tongue to dance with his. His body responded instantly and he grasped her right hip, bringing her hard against him. He said her name on a kind of agonized whisper, running his other hand down her back. The zipper on her dress teased his fingertips and he edged it down slowly, inch by torturous inch. She moaned low in her throat when his palm splayed across her bare back and he realized she wore no bra, which drugged him senseless.

"Kayla," he said raggedly against her lips. "Let's go back to the house. If I don't make love to you soon I think I'll go crazy."

"No," she said and pressed against him, drawing his mouth to hers again.

"No?" he queried, confused by the mixed signals.

"Let's stay here," she replied, breathless. "I want this. Now."

The urgency and longing in her voice in that moment

made it impossible for Liam to deny her anything. He kissed her again. Hotter and harder, over and over, until he could take no more and he scooped her up into his arms and lifted her into the boat and laid her down on the small bed in the cabin. He chucked off his shirt and shoes and pulled the sandals from her feet in about twenty of the longest seconds of his life.

Then he kissed her again. And again. And gently tugged the dress straps off her shoulders, exposing her perfect breasts. He cupped them softly, rubbing the hard, rosy nipples with his thumbs and she groaned with a kind of heady pleasure that fueled his longing for her like gasoline on a bonfire. Her hands were at his nape, in his hair, on his shoulders, each touch more encouraging than the last. He bent his head and kissed her breasts, first one, then the other, taking each nipple into his mouth in turn, circling the hard peaks with his tongue. She arched and moaned again, pressing closer, gripping tighter, running her hands over him everywhere she could reach.

Liam managed to peel the dress off in between possessing her beautiful mouth and when he stripped her lace briefs down her hips he realized his hands were shaking. Crazy. He'd seen her naked countless times. He'd stroked and loved every inch of her smooth skin. But she still had the power to make him mindless. He trailed his mouth over her breasts, down her rib cage and across her belly. He lingered there for a moment, scrolling his tongue around the edge of her navel in the way he knew she liked. Then he went lower, encouraged by her soft moans, and kissed her intimately. Her thighs quivered and he held her steady, taking his time to draw every ounce of response from her. The taste of her pushed his desire, drove him on to make her come apart. She groaned, she writhed, she said his name over and then Liam felt her tip over the edge. Driven by the onslaught of his mouth and hands, she climaxed in a white-hot rush that was blisteringly erotic and like an addictive, narcotic high to every sense he possessed.

Kayla came back down to earth, shattered and so gratified she couldn't manage to do anything for a moment but lie limp and try to recapture her breath. He moved up beside her, his hands sliding over her skin in a way that was sinfully sensual and heightened her need to feel him above her, around her and then inside her.

She reached for him, tugging at the waistband of his jeans. "Take these off," she said and rolled a little, pressing her mouth to his chest.

"I guess we don't need to worry about birth control," he said, chuckling as he dragged off the rest of his clothes.

Kayla gripped his shoulders. "Not for a while."

"Just as well, since it's up at the house," he said and pressed one leg between her thighs.

Kayla smiled and lifted her hips in silent invitation. He complied immediately, entering her, possessing her lips in a demanding kiss as he possessed her body. She moved, accepting him inside, and then wrapped her legs around him. Locked together in the most intimate way possible, he began to move. She matched him, met him, felt the way he filled her and completed her like no other man ever had. And he took his time, back and forth, creating an erotic, steady rhythm in between deep, wet kisses that rendered her breathless and then utterly and completely *his*.

They came within moments of each other. Kayla first, up and over an incredible high of pleasure, her entire body pulsing with an orgasm that was so torturously intense it almost numbed her senses. When he followed she gripped his hips, holding on, feeling every shudder, every muscle he possessed tense and burn like an inferno as release claimed him.

When their breathing returned to normal he rolled off her and lay at her side on the small bed. It was a cramped space, but she didn't mind. He took hold of her hand and brought her knuckles to his mouth, kissing her softly.

"Are you okay?"

"Yes," she breathed contentedly. "It was perfect."

He chuckled. "You're easy on me. We'll try this again later," he promised. "I'll take more time and use a little more finesse."

"I'm the one who didn't want to waste time going back to the house," she reminded him and traced her fingers over his ribcage. His hand covered hers and she felt the cool gold wedding band slide across her knuckles. "You wear this all the time now," she said and rubbed the band with one finger.

His chest expanded. "I've kept it on since we found out about the baby."

Kayla glanced guiltily at her bare left hand. It was exactly the sort of thing he would do. The right thing. Typically Liam. Honor and truth above all else. His wedding band was a way of honoring the child she carried. "I'm sorry… I haven't made much of an effort at this marriage."

"No, you haven't."

She laughed humorlessly. "God, Liam, don't you *ever* lie…not even to make me feel better?"

She heard his chest rumble. "Nope. Not ever."

"Don't I know it," Kayla said and sat up, suddenly and foolishly conscious of her nudity. "Can you pass me my clothes?"

He reached across the small bed to retrieve her dress and briefs and was back in his jeans and T-shirt before she'd managed to slip the dress over her head. "Now who's sulking," he remarked as she huffed when the zipper got caught.

"Jerk," she muttered and slid off the bed. She grabbed her sandals and glared at him. "Can you help me down?"

He laughed, scooped her up effortlessly and within a minute she was trudging her way back up to the house. He wasn't far behind and by the time she'd slammed a couple of doors he was laughing again.

"You know," he said when she was back in her bedroom and ditching her shoes, "you shouldn't ask a question if you don't want to hear the answer."

He was by the door, arms crossed, looking way too self-satisfied. Well, she'd practically jumped his bones with a little encouragement, so the look on his face wasn't unexpected. If she'd had something to throw at him, she would have! Smug, condescending, ass.

"Don't let the door hit you on the way out," she said tartly.

He laughed and gave her a look that was scorching hot. "I gotta say," he said and took a few steps across the room, "that I'm really turned on right now."

Kayla grabbed a slipper from the end of the bed and tossed it in his direction. But his reflexes were so acute he caught it midair. "You don't get to tell me I'm a lousy wife in one sentence and then look at me all sexy with those blue eyes of yours."

"Actually," he said and walked around the huge bed, "I'm pretty sure I do."

He caught up with her in two strides and then she was in his arms. He kissed her, harder than usual, more demanding, and without any resistance, she kissed him back, matching every slant, every slide of his tongue in her mouth. Within a minute their clothes were off again and they were on the bed, making love in a kind of frenzied haze. No words. No foreplay. Just possession. Just flesh to flesh, skin to skin. Just Liam's strong body over her, around her and inside her, taking and giving, arousing her more with each erotic stroke. Release was powerful and quick, shuttling them both up and over into a vortex of pleasure that was mind-blowingly intense.

Afterward, they lay on their sides, breathing hard, their limbs tangled up with rumpled bedsheets. She heard him chuckle, but was too weary to raise her head from his chest.

"So much for finesse," he said. "You turn my good intentions to mush, Mrs. O'Sullivan."

Kayla stiffened immediately. It was the first time he'd called her that. The first time *anyone* had called her that. Shame licked at her heels. She really was a rotten wife. She hoped she'd be a better mother. The thought rolled around in her head. So much had happened in the last few days that she'd spent very little time thinking about her baby, she acknowledged shamefully. *My baby.* Her hand dropped to her belly and she felt a deep, abiding love for the child she carried that was so intense it was almost painful.

"I'm going to be a mom," she said quietly.

Liam rolled, reaching out to cover her hand with his own. "You'll be amazing."

Her chest tightened. "You, too. Do you have a preference? I mean, a boy or a girl?"

"Nope," he replied and spread his hand wider, smoothing it across her skin. "I'm happy either way."

They chatted about the baby and laughed over possible names. It was the first real conversation they'd had about their child and she felt the connection between them through to her bones. They'd spent so much time arguing about everything else, they hadn't spent any time thinking about what was really important. *Their baby.*

"You're really happy about this? About the baby, I mean?" she asked and rolled onto her side.

Liam did the same and then gently cradled her head in one hand. "Absolutely."

"Even though everything else is—"

"Yes," he said and pressed a finger to her lips. "Even then. There is something we need to do, though. Something important."

"What's that?"

"Go and see you parents again. Together."

"No, I—"

"You're unhappy," he said, cutting her off. "And that's not acceptable to me. We need to sort this out. You need to make peace with them, or with yourself over this. Pretending there isn't a problem won't help."

"I'm not," she said defiantly as opposition surged through her. "I don't think that's a good idea. I need to talk with them alone first. My dad—"

"Your dad needs to see that we are unified in this, Kayla. How do you expect them to respect our relationship if you don't?"

It was a direct hit. And a painful one. "You don't understand."

She pulled away and sat up, grabbing the robe on the end of the bed. She slipped it on and belted her waist, very aware that Liam had hardly moved. She glanced over her shoulder, saw the heat in his gaze and got to her feet.

"I understand perfectly," he said and sprang off the bed and quickly pulled his jeans on, leaving the snap undone. "You don't wear my ring, you don't have my name...the message isn't subliminal, is it?"

Annoyance seeped through her blood. His ring. His name. His words had arrogance written all over them. "If this about your ego being somehow deflated because I haven't—"

"A bomb wouldn't deflate my ego," he said roughly. "This isn't about ego. It's about you and me…about the vows we took. Love, honor and cherish, remember? Those words meant something to me, Kayla. So, maybe there was too much champagne that weekend and maybe the preacher was dressed like Elvis…but it was still *real*."

The frustration in his voice was unmistakable. "It was real to me, too."

"Then prove it."

"I shouldn't have to," she shot back, tugging at the belt around her waist. "If you love me you'll—"

"If?" he echoed, cutting her off. *"If I love you?"* He ran an exasperated hand through his hair, staring at her, his blue eyes dark and intense. His next words were ragged and raspy. "Sometimes…sometimes you say the most damnable things. You're killing me here, you know that?"

Then he strode from the room without saying anything else.

Kayla slumped back onto the bed, hurting all over. Their fledgling marriage was in crisis and she knew she needed to do something about it. Only she had no idea what that was.

Chapter Nine

"So, she's serious about the divorce?"

Liam focussed his attention on his brother. Kieran had flown into Rapid City airport that morning and hired a rental car for the forty-minute drive to Cedar River. Now they were sitting in Liam's office at the hotel and drinking coffee.

"So it would seem," he replied, fighting the twitch in his gut and the pain at his temple. It seemed as though he'd had a headache for days. But not one that painkillers would ease. It was only one o'clock on Wednesday afternoon, but he felt like downing a few belts of scotch to numb his senses.

His brother shook his head. "Have you tried talking with her?"

"Mom's not listening to me," he said flatly. "Maybe you'll have more luck."

"I'll go and see her this afternoon," Kieran said and

shrugged. "Once I hear about this mess direct from the old man."

"He's not denying it," Liam flipped back. "Not anymore. And I think he's accepted the inevitable."

Kieran shook his head. "Damn. So, how are things with you and Kayla?"

I have no idea...

Which wasn't exactly true. The last four days had been tense. Oh, they went through the motions—breakfast conversation, a cursory kiss on the cheek before they went to sleep at night and a brief call during the day to see how she was. But that was it. The tension between them was acute and palpable. Since their argument after those incredibly passionate couple of hours on Saturday afternoon, they were more like barely tolerated roommates than husband and wife. She made sure she was in bed well before he turned in and was up before his alarm buzzed at six. There was no companionship, no affection and definitely no making love. Having her so close, but feeling the distance between them getting wider and wider every day, was the worst kind of torture.

"Fine," he said, answering his brother's question. "How about you?"

Kieran looked less than his usual positive self. His brother had been through his own brand of marital crap over a year ago, when his wife had announced that the son he believed was his, was in fact the child of his best friend. He'd raised the boy as his own for eighteen months and Liam couldn't even begin to comprehend the kind of hurt his younger brother must have felt by such an unforgivable betrayal.

"Same," he said and shrugged. "Work and more work."

"Dating?"

"Hell, no," Kieran said quickly. "I'm off that merry-go-round for a while."

"You know, Nicola Radici has moved back to town," he said and smiled. "She's taken over JoJo's since her brother and his wife were killed in that plane crash last year." Nicola was Kieran's high school girlfriend, the one he'd left behind. "She's also caring for her two young nephews now."

Kieran's expression was like granite. "Nic and I were over a long time ago."

Liam shrugged. "Worth a thought."

"No chance. Nicola hates me. You do remember how badly I screwed up with her?"

"You were young. When we're young we do stupid things."

"Except for you," Kieran said and grinned. "You never wavered back then. Looks like you saved your stupid thing for now."

"Are you trying to make a point?" he asked, irritated, frustrated and already tired of the conversation. "If so, get to it."

"All I'm saying is that this thing with you and Kayla kind of came out of left field. Was it the hands-off instruction from the old man when we were growing up that made you do it? I mean, she's beautiful and smart and sexy and—"

"And my *wife*, remember?" he said roughly. "So enough with the compliments, okay?"

Kieran's eyes bulged and then he chuckled. "Well, I'll be damned...you really love her. Congratulations, by the way...about the baby."

He was about to thank his brother when their father walked into the office. He hugged Kieran, gave Liam a nod and then dropped into one of the chairs. He'd spoken to his father only once during the past couple of days and that conversation had been curt. He certainly didn't want to be at war with his parent, but loyalty toward his mother kept him guarded.

They talked for a while, about their mom, about Sean, about Liz and her three little girls. They reminisced about their childhood and some of Sean's antics when he was a teenager, and not once did they mention their now not-so-secret half brother, even though he suspected the usually curious Kieran was itching to know more about the man who shared their blood, but was a stranger to them.

"I'm going to go and see Mom," Kieran said a while later and got to his feet. "I'll catch you both later."

Once his brother left the room, Liam put in a call to Connie and gave her a short list of things he needed done that afternoon. When he was done with the call he looked up and noticed his father hadn't moved.

"Are we gonna have this out?" J.D. asked, both brows up.

"Is there any point?"

"You've got questions…only natural."

"Kieran's the curious one, not me," Liam supplied and flicked on his laptop.

"I'm not saying this to Kieran. I'm saying it to you. Tell me what you want to know."

Liam almost got to his feet and left the room. *Almost.* He took a deep breath and met his father's gaze. "Okay… just one question…why did you do it?"

"Why did I fall in love with Kathleen Rickard?" he shot back. "Why did I fall for the one woman I knew I shouldn't want? You tell me," he said and laughed humorlessly. "It looks like the apple doesn't fall far from the tree."

Liam scowled. "It's not the same thing," he said. "You cheated on your wife with a younger woman. You got her pregnant and then ran her out of town so you wouldn't get caught."

"I didn't…" His father's voice trailed off. "It was a long time ago. Can't we just leave it to rest?"

"You have a son with this woman," Liam reminded him.

"A son who hates me," his father said, clearly pained by the reality. "A son who doesn't want to see me. Who's never wanted to see me. A son who has spent his entire life pushing me away and refuses to acknowledge that I'm his father. A son who I have to *let* hate me, because as his father, it's the only thing I can actually do for him."

His father's eyes were shining, and it reminded Liam that the only time he'd ever witnessed real emotion from the man was when Liz had died. And right now, in this moment.

"Did you ever love Mom?" Liam asked quietly.

J.D. sighed heavily. "She was a good wife to me. What I needed back then. I'd just taken over the business from your grandfather. I was busy and your mom understood that. She understood me."

"That wasn't the question."

"I love that we've had a long marriage. I love that she gifted me with four incredible children. But…no, I was never in love with her like I should have been. Like she deserved."

"Like you were with Kathleen?"

"Yes," his father admitted. "And I know you probably don't believe me and it doesn't really matter now, but my relationship with Kathleen ended the day she left town. And yes, I supported her and Jonah and I would visit so I could see my son, but the affair ended thirty years ago and I have been faithful to your mother ever since."

"Mom's going to divorce you…you know that, right?"

His father nodded slowly. "What about you, Liam? Are you going to stay angry with me? You're my eldest son and more than that…we've always been friends, you and

I. More so than with your brothers. I hope you can learn to forgive me."

"Me, too, Dad," he said and let out a heavy sigh. "Me, too."

Kayla wasn't sure what kind of reception she'd get when she tapped on her parents' door on Wednesday afternoon. Icy, she suspected. She'd called an hour earlier and left a message, saying she was dropping by. Her mother answered the door and guilt almost stripped her bare when she noticed how tired and unwell she seemed. There were dark circles beneath her mother's eyes and her complexion was pale and tight.

She walked down the hall and into the living room. Her grandmother, Joyce, was sitting by the window in her favorite chair and Kayla immediately moved forward and gave her a loving hug.

"Hi, Grams."

"You look tired," her grandmother said. "Not sleeping well?"

No. Because I spend most of the night trying desperately not to roll over to Liam's side of the bed in case I ended up cradled in his arms. Even though that's the one place I want to be.

It had been a long and difficult few days. They lived together, but were as far apart as two people could be. They had hardly spoken for days; instead they passed each other in the morning and evening, barely acknowledging that they were in the middle of a crisis. Other than a perfunctory kiss good-night, he didn't touch her and she didn't invite him to. They talked about the weather, the upcoming benefit and the baby and everything else was ignored.

"I'm fine, Grams. You?"

"Old," she replied and grinned a little. "Tired."

"I'm sorry I haven't been to see you sooner," she said and hugged her grandmother again. "I miss you."

"Kayla?"

Her father's voice made her swivel around. He stood near the door, arms crossed, his glasses perched on the edge of his nose in a way that was familiar and endearing. "Hi, Dad."

"Are you here to tell us you've come to your senses?"

Okay, first hurdle. "I wanted to talk with you and Mom."

"About O'Sullivan?" he asked and scowled. "Because I'm not interested in hearing about him."

"I'm not here to talk about Liam," she said and saw her father wince at the mention of his name. "I want to talk about you. About you and me and Mom and Grams. And about how we used to be a family and now we're—"

"Your doing," he said harshly, cutting her off. "You chose him. Over us. Over your family that has always loved you."

It sounded so final. So…absolute.

Kayla's eyes burned. "Are you never going to make peace with this, Dad?"

His expression softened for a moment and she saw him swallow hard. "You broke my heart. You broke your mother's heart. And your grandmother…" His words trailed off. "I lost my sister because of those people…because J.D. couldn't stay faithful to his wife. He took my sister from her family. And now his son has done the same thing with my daughter."

"But I'm still here, Dad. I'm *still* your daughter. My marriage to Liam doesn't have to change that. And once you get to know him, you'll see that he's—"

"I don't want any O'Sullivans in my house!"

Her father's harsh tone made her cringe. And when she noticed her grandmother was crying, Kayla's heart constricted in her chest. Her mother moved across the room to comfort the older woman, and Kayla remained where she was, heartsick.

She touched her abdomen. "What about your grandchild? This baby is half O'Sullivan... I can't change that. And I want my child to have you in their life. I want my child to be a part of this family."

"One day you'll understand the hurt I feel," her father said in a raspy voice. "You'll understand this betrayal when your child does something so callous to you. You're my beautiful and smart daughter and we've always been proud of you...and you could have had any man you wanted. Why him? Why O'Sullivan's son? When you knew what it would do to us."

Kayla swallowed back the excruciating pain in her throat. "I didn't plan this. It just happened. We fell in love," she whispered, suddenly wishing and longing for Liam's strength beside her. He'd wanted to come with her. A united front, he'd said. But she'd pushed him away. Again. "*I* fell in love."

The words seemed to physically hurt her father. "So did Kathleen. And then she left. She left us and could never look back."

"It was a different time, Dad. A different situation. And now that everything is out in the open, things will be better. Mr. and Mrs. O'Sullivan are—"

"Nothing will be better. You'll still be married to *him* and Kathleen will still be living in Oregon. Do you know what we get now? What your grandmother gets? A Christmas card. That's all. A lousy card that we've never been able to display because it would cause too many questions. It's like we had to wipe my sister from our lives and pretend she didn't exist for thirty years. All because J.D. wasn't man enough to be faithful to his wife."

"I think he loved her," Kayla said quietly, hurting all over. "I think he loved Kathleen."

"Those people don't know the meaning of the word," her father spat back. "They know about being rich and entitled and arrogant and how to bulldoze their way through life to get what they want... But love?" He shook his head. "They don't have the spine for it. I'm sure you'll find that out the hard way. Because I can't imagine that your new *husband* is all that different from his old man. He'll hurt you. He'll betray you. He'll cheat on you."

"If you would just give him a chance..."

"I can't," her father said. "I could, for anyone but him. Men like that don't know how to stay faithful. It's in his genes to hurt and betray people. I only hope you have the sense to get out before he does that to you."

He refused to say another word to her, so after kissing her grandmother goodbye and exchanging a sad look with her mother, she left and headed straight home. It was only three o'clock, but she didn't have the energy to go back to the museum. There was a missed call from Liam on her cell and she texted back that she was tired and was heading home. She called Shirley to cover her shift for the afternoon and drove back to the house. Ash called, but she wasn't in the mood for a heart-to-heart with her friend, either. Instead she stripped off her clothes, took a hot shower and dressed in pink pajamas with ducks on them and sat on the couch, flicking through a magazine. Which was where Liam found her when he arrived home just after five.

"Everything all right?" he asked and dropped his keys and cell on the coffee table.

"Fine," she said and closed the magazine.

"A bit early for pj's?"

She shrugged. "I'm having a pity party."

"Am I invited?"

"It's not like I have a choice," she said and sighed. "We live together."

"Do we?" he shot back. "Seems to me that we're about as far apart as two people could possibly be."

She looked up and met his gaze. "Do you want me to move back to my apartment?"

The silence between them was suddenly deafening. His blue eyes darkened and he held out his hands. "Is that what you want? Are you trying to break me down, Kayla? To see what it will take to have me on my knees?"

There was real pain in his voice and shame immediately filled her blood. "No… I'm sorry. I'm just… I saw my parents today."

He went perfectly still. "And?"

"And my father thinks you're going to do to me what your dad did to your mom." When he didn't respond, she continued. "Cheat. Be unfaithful."

A pulse throbbed in his cheek. "Does that seem likely?"

"Not at all," she replied. "I don't think you have a dishonorable bone in your body."

His gaze was unwavering. "Did you tell him that?"

"He's not exactly listening to me at the moment." She shrugged and sighed heavily. "Liam, there's something I want to do, and I'll understand if you don't agree…but I need to do it."

He immediately looked cautious—and curious. "What?"

"I want to go to Oregon," she said quietly. "I want to see my aunt and find out what really happened thirty years ago."

Liam stood rigid, clearly absorbing her announcement. Silence stretched like elastic between them, as though he was thinking of every possible reason why she shouldn't go. And then he spoke.

"I'll book our flight."

* * *

Liam had never been to Portland. And with rain that hadn't eased for hours, he figured he might never again. It was Friday morning and Kayla was sitting beside him in the rental car, muttering directions she'd found via the GPS on her cell.

They'd arrived that morning, checked into a hotel in the center of town and headed to Kathleen Rickard's home. J.D. had supplied the address, which was about a twenty-minute drive out of the city. The area was neat and the homes large and he pushed back the niggling feeling of resentment in his gut, knowing his father had probably bought the house for his secret family.

They pulled up outside a two-story, redbrick home with white gables, a wide porch and large front yard. There was a tire swing tied to a tree and he vaguely wondered if his father had put the rope there years earlier. It reminded Liam of the rope swing J.D. had hung from the old oak tree behind the barn at the ranch when he was a boy.

"Let's go," he said an unbuckled his seat belt.

By the time he'd grabbed the umbrella from the back and gotten out from the car, Kayla had her door open and was stepping onto the curb. Liam held the umbrella over her head and ignored the rain falling onto his shoulders. He opened the white gate and they walked up the path to the porch. There were four steps and he ushered Kayla forward, keeping her covered. Once they were underneath the porch and out of the rain, he shook the umbrella and moved to knock on the door. But the door opened before he had a chance.

A woman greeted them. Tall and slender, she was about fifty years old and had a soft, blond bob. She was very beautiful, the kind of beauty that wouldn't fade with years. In fact, it was remarkable how much Kayla looked like her.

They shared the same soft brown eyes, slanted brows and high cheek bones.

"Can I help you?" she asked, frowning and then he noticed how her gaze quickly softened.

He cleared his throat. "Ms. Rickard, I'm—"

"I know who you are," she said and waved a hand gently. "I was your babysitter once, Liam," she reminded him. "And I've seen your photograph many times." She looked toward Kayla. "And you must be my niece? J.D. called my son this week and told him you had both recently married. Congratulations."

Kayla nodded. "Thank you…Aunt Kathleen."

Her expression softened. "Why don't you come in out of this rain and tell me what I can do for you," she said and opened the door.

Within half a minute they were in a comfy living room, seated on a wide chintz sofa. There was an easel in the corner and canvases scattered around the room.

"You're an artist?" Kayla said, clearly intrigued.

"Of sorts. I like to paint," Kathleen said as she sat in the seat opposite. "But I don't imagine you've come all this way to discuss my painting. What can I do for you?"

Liam saw Kayla's chin wobble and he grasped her hand. "We'd like to know what happened between you and my father."

A look of surprise crossed her face. "Don't you know?"

"Your version," Liam qualified. "Unabridged."

She rested her hands on her knees and sighed. "I'd like to let my son know that you're here," she said quietly. "And then I'll tell you what you want to know." She took a few moments to send a text message and then returned her attention to them. "Okay, here's my version—I fell in love with a married man." She met Liam's gaze head-on. "Are you sure you want to hear this?"

He nodded. "*We* need to know."

She nodded and began to speak. In his rage and resentment, Liam knew he'd been expecting a tawdry, impossibly inappropriate story about how his father had seduced a younger woman and once she was pregnant, paid her off and shuttled her out of town. But Kathleen Rickard's version of events was nothing so scandalous. She was young, she fell in love with a married man who was twelve years older and they had tried to fight their feelings for months. And once she discovered she was expecting a baby, it was *Kathleen* who had insisted she leave town, not his father.

"He wanted to tell your mother, to make things right. But I wouldn't allow it," she said with a kind of admirable strength. "He had a young family and a wife who deserved to have her family stay together. I wasn't going to be a home-wrecker. So I left town...of my own will. And to make it easier for me to make the break from my family and my much older and overprotective brother, J.D. let everyone think he'd made me go." She let out a long sigh. "Look, we made a lot of mistakes back then. I had no right to get involved with a married man...but I was young and foolish and even though it's no excuse, I simply followed my heart."

I simply followed my heart.

Damn...if only it were that simple.

He squeezed Kayla's hand and spoke. "My father told me the affair was over the day you left...is that true?"

"Yes. I learned from my mistake. And frankly, once I'd left South Dakota, all I wanted to do was have my baby and raise him the best I could. But your father didn't abandon us," she stressed. "He wanted to be a part of my son's life. He still does. But Jonah..." Her words trailed off and she sighed a little sadly. "Jonah is stubborn and headstrong. Does that sound familiar?" she asked and smiled.

Liam's mouth twitched and as much as he hadn't planned on it, he realized it was damned difficult not to like and respect Kathleen Rickard.

Kayla's fingers were numb from Liam squeezing her hand, but she didn't pull away. She knew how tough the situation was for him and she admired how he held it together as they spoke to her aunt. And she liked Kathleen. The other woman was frank and forthright and clearly led a happy and productive life, even if there was a little sadness in her eyes when she spoke about J.D. and her son.

They chatted for a while and were just settling down to drink the coffee she'd brewed—along with a tea she'd made for Kayla—when the front door opened and then slammed and footsteps came down the hall. And then, there he was— Jonah Rickard—framing the doorway. Six foot something of dark-haired, angry handsomeness. Kayla gasped when he appeared, because he looked so much like Liam. His hair was a little darker, his shoulders a little leaner, but the glittering blue eyes and strong jaw were pure O'Sullivan.

Liam sprang to his feet and looked ready to face whatever was to come of this first meeting between him and his brother. Jonah didn't look happy—not one bit—and Kayla suspected that was probably a common thing for him. He was livid and not bothering to hide it. So, he was another bastion of truth, another righter of wrongs and another man who lived by a code of black and white without shades of gray, she thought and smiled to herself.

"Jonah," Kathleen said as she stood, clearly ready to defuse the escalating tension simmering between the two men who had yet to say something to one another. "I'm so pleased you had the time to stop by. I have visitors."

"So I see."

Oh, yeah, he was mad. Seething in fact. As though some

kind of predator had invaded his territory and needed sorting out. Kayla realized that he would do whatever he had to do to protect the woman who had given him life. They were a tight unit. A family. And he looked ready to fight, with his taut fists and locked shoulders.

"Which one are you?" Jonah asked, one brow up. "The doctor? Mr. Hollywood?"

Kayla glanced at Liam, saw that he looked remarkably at ease by his brother's unexpected appearance and then felt a powerful surge of respect flow through her. He wouldn't lose control. He wouldn't make a scene. He had a kind of dignified control in his profile and it made her love him all the more. He was a rock. Solid. A man who could handle anything. *My husband.* She experienced an almost silly gush of happiness and grasped his forearm, digging her fingertips in and latching on tight.

"Neither," Liam said quietly.

"Ah," Jonah said with a kind of chilling mockery. "The big gun himself. The favored eldest child of J.D. O'Sullivan is gracing us with his presence. My life is complete."

"It's good to meet you," Liam replied, clearly choosing to ignore the other man's sarcasm.

"Is it?" Jonah shot back. "Did the old man put you up to this?"

"No," Liam said quietly.

"Then why are you here?" Jonah asked, his mouth then pressed into a thin, tense line.

Liam half shrugged and Kayla suspected he did it to antagonize the other man just a little. "My wife wanted to meet you. And I was…curious."

Jonah scowled, confirming Kayla's suspicions that he harbored a whole lot of resentment—most of it aimed at anyone named O'Sullivan.

"Well," Kathleen said and gave a soft, almost brittle laugh. "Why don't we all sit down and talk?"

"I think I'll pass, Mom."

"You might want to hear this, Jonah."

"Hear what?" he demanded.

The older woman offered a tight smile. "That I've decided that I'm going on a trip."

"To where?" he asked.

Kathleen pushed back her shoulders with a resilient sigh. "To South Dakota. I think it's time I went home."

Chapter Ten

Kayla wasn't sure what to expect from the reunion between her father and Kathleen. Especially since sourpuss Jonah had made it very clear he didn't want anything to do with *anyone*. Her family included. He was only coming to Cedar River to keep a protective and watchful eye over his beloved mother. End of story.

He refused any offer to be collected at the airport in Rapid City, choosing to hire a car and drive to Cedar River. By the time the rental car pulled up outside her parents' home on Monday, Kayla had watched her father's mood shift between anticipation and despair as the afternoon stretched on. But her concerns evaporated once she witnessed her grandmother's joy at being reunited with her daughter and then finally meeting her grandson. To his relief, Jonah wasn't completely disagreeable and appeared to be making an effort to be civil. Her father cried a little when he hugged Kathleen for the first time in three decades and

Kayla had to wipe a few tears from her own eyes. It was an emotional moment for everyone. And yet, oddly, she had a niggling feeling of disconnect as she watched her family together. And she felt...alone. And missing Liam more than she'd thought possible. But there was no way her father would have agreed to him being there.

Once everyone was settled in the living room, Kayla headed to the kitchen to make tea. With Jonah right behind her.

"Where's the big gun?" he asked, lingering in the doorway.

Kayla knew exactly who he was talking about and ignored his cynical tone. "Liam's at the hotel. Where you're staying while you're in town."

He shrugged lightly and looked around. "Mom's decided she wants to stay here."

"But not you?" she queried, one brow arched.

He shrugged again. "She needs some space to reconnect with everyone."

She suspected the only person needing space was Jonah Rickard. Still, despite his scowl and disagreeable tone, she couldn't help feeling compassion for him.

"Grams is so happy that you and your mom are here. By the way, you should start calling her Grams right away...it will hurt her feelings if you don't," Kayla said and smiled sweetly.

"I don't think I—"

"You and I are her only grandchildren," she said pointedly. "That might be something to think about while you're sitting all alone in your hotel room."

He frowned. "This isn't some kind of happy family reunion for me, *cousin*. I'm here to make sure my mother is—"

"I know why you're here," Kayla said, cutting him off.

"To protect your mom. I get that. I feel the same way about my parents."

"Is that why you married a man they hate?"

Kayla didn't respond. Jonah Rickard's issues were his own and she had enough to think about without getting mad at him for trying to bait her. Besides, it wasn't a question she could answer without digging deep into her fractured relationship with her husband. Things had remained on ice since they'd returned from Portland and they hadn't discussed what Kathleen's and Jonah's arrival would do to the dynamic of both their families. And their marriage. But she knew it wasn't a conversation they could avoid indefinitely.

"You know, if it's all too much having Kieran and Jonah at the hotel, as well as your father, your dad could stay here?" Kayla suggested on Wednesday morning.

They were in the kitchen. Liam was making coffee and Kayla was buttering toast.

"I think Dad would prefer to be at the hotel," Liam replied, dropping a tea bag into her favorite mug, "to make sure he doesn't cause any trouble."

He.

Jonah.

"Have you tried talking to him?" she asked as she returned the butter to the refrigerator.

"I talked to my father yesterday."

"I meant Jonah," she said. "I mean, he is your brother and—"

"Half brother," he corrected. "And talking to him makes my teeth hurt."

She chuckled, amazed at how good it felt. "It's just that he's probably feeling a little caged right now, with his mom being here and reconnecting with my parents...and also left out. It wouldn't hurt to try."

"No."

Kayla dropped a loaf of sourdough bread on the counter. "God, you can be so stubborn about some things."

He came around the counter and stood beside her, reaching out to push a lock of hair back from her face. He wore a strained expression, almost as though he was touching her against his will. "I know."

"He's still your brother," she reminded him. "Half or otherwise. I'm sure you would have had a chance since he's staying at the hotel."

"The hotel doesn't run itself," he said roughly. "And I'm not about to start babysitting that surly—"

"How's your mom?" she asked quickly, cutting him off. "Any more talk about the...you know?"

He dropped his hand. "The divorce? No. But I don't think it's up for negotiation. She seems determined to go through with it."

Kayla resisted the urge to touch him. "She still might change her mind. She's hurting and people do and say things they don't mean when they're in pain. Like Jonah," she added.

"Are you his number one fan all of a sudden?"

He actually sounded jealous! Kayla scowled. "You could make more of an effort with him, for your dad's sake."

"So could he. I'm certain he did all he could to avoid me yesterday. And Kieran."

She sighed heavily. "Maybe he's scared to try. You *can* be a bit intimidating at times."

"Actually, I'm pretty sure my half brother isn't intimidated by anything or anyone. He's a sullen, bad-tempered brat who's probably been overindulged by his mother all his life and is now skulking around my hotel snarling at anyone who looks in his direction." He shrugged lightly, indicating that the conversation about his brother was over.

But Kayla wasn't done. "Maybe he just needs a hug or something?"

Liam's brows shot up immediately. "Yeah…right. More like a punch in those perfectly straight teeth."

Kayla propped her hands on her hips. "Are you jealous that's he's here? Is that it?"

"Jealous?" he echoed. "Of what?"

"Of his relationship with your father."

"He doesn't have a relationship with my father," Liam shot back. "And I'm not ten years old. I stopped looking for my dad's attention and approval a long time ago. Some of us grow up, you know."

It was a low blow. And deliberately aimed at her and what he considered her codependent relationship with her parents. "Did you get out on the mean side of the bed this morning?" she said, defiant, and then backtracked a little when she saw the gleam in his eye. In dark trousers and pale blue shirt matched with an even bluer tie, he looked effortlessly sexy. "Not that I'd know. Because…well…I have been sleeping alone this week."

Because Liam had taken to sleeping in the downstairs bedroom. It wasn't that she'd kicked him out of their bed. It was all his doing. When she asked him why, he'd muttered something about how restless she was while she slept and he was giving her room to get a better night's sleep. Which he insisted she needed because she was pregnant. Of course, she wasn't buying into his excuse. Not one iota.

He was angry. Plain and simple.

There was a black cloud of rage around him that seemed to be getting darker every day. But he was also doing his best to disguise the fact because he was honorable and thoughtful and didn't want to upset her. In fact, he was *so* thoughtful he was driving her crazy. Nothing was too much trouble…her favorite food, her favorite television shows; he'd even offered to run a scented bath and rub her feet. There were flowers sitting in a vase in the hallway and an uneaten box of chocolates in the refrigerator.

"You need your rest, doctor's orders," he said and unexpectedly laid a hand on her belly.

"You're fussing like an old woman."

"You're having my baby, so I'm allowed," he said quietly. "I wonder when you'll start showing."

"Soon enough," she said and ignored the heat traveling over her skin. It was the closest they'd been in days and she missed his touch. "I'm only about eight weeks along. But other than the relentless fatigue, I feel good. Not much morning sickness. I still have a few cravings and I do always seem to be hungry these days."

"Sometimes," he said and gently palmed her abdomen. "Sometimes, amid all the craziness with our families, I think we can forget that in seven months' time we're going to be parents. Which means we should probably start thinking about turning one of the bedrooms into a nursery. If we know the baby's sex you can decorate to your heart's content."

"We can find out the sex when I have my first ultrasound. Unless you'd rather be surprised?"

He shrugged. "I don't need to know. I just want us to have a healthy baby. But if you want to find out I'll—"

"I think I do want to know," she said and covered his hand with hers. "That way we can start picking names."

"Jack," he suggested and half smiled. "For a boy."

Kayla liked that. Jack was her grandfather's name. She stroked his fingertips. "And for a girl, Beth," she said and swallowed the inexplicable lump in the throat. "After your sister."

His eyes suddenly glittered and looked bluer than she'd

ever seen them. "My mom would like that, I'm sure. It's a sweet gesture. Thank you."

"Jack O'Sullivan. Beth O'Sullivan. Both have a nice feel to them."

His gaze narrowed. "O'Sullivan?"

The query in his voice was unmistakable. "Of course."

"It's hard to know what your plans are," he said and grabbed her left hand, gently caressing her bare finger. "Considering you still don't wear the ring I bought you."

She winced and did her utmost to ignore the controlled resentment in his voice. "Um... I'm going to go and see my parents again after work today."

"Okay," he said easily. "I'll pick you up and we'll—"

"It's better if I go alone," she said quickly. "And maybe stay for dinner. With my aunt and possibly Jonah being there...I don't want to upset my father and Grams hasn't been feeling well and—"

"I get it, Kayla," he said quietly, dropping his hand. "You want to spend some time with your family. Alone. So, go." Liam walked around the counter and grabbed his coffee mug, drinking the contents before placing it back on the counter. He grabbed his jacket from the back of a chair, picked up his keys and gave her a cursory nod. "I'll be at the office late. Don't wait up."

He was out the room and the house before she had a chance to respond. Every conversation they had was fraught with bitterness and misunderstanding. They lived together, but lived apart. His words still echoed in her head.

You still don't wear the ring I bought you...

She'd thought about slipping the beautiful platinum-and-diamond band onto her finger countless times over the past week. But every time she considered it, something held her back. She wasn't sure what. Thinking about it made her head hurt.

Kayla left not long after and arrived at the museum a little before eight thirty. She had a full day planned. With the benefit only a few days away there were several last-minute details she needed to see to, including meeting with two of the guest artists. Plus, she had to go and pick up her gown and shoes from the boutique down the street.

Ash dropped by around lunchtime with a roasted pepper and cream cheese bagel and she spent half an hour chatting with her friend.

"I think I am seriously starting to eat for two," she said and patted her belly once she'd eaten the last of the sandwich. "I'll be sniffing around the vending machine in the staffroom by three o'clock."

Ash grinned. "I can't believe I'm going to say this, but being pregnant makes you look even more beautiful. As if that were really possible."

"Except for the bags under my eyes from lack of sleep," she said ruefully. "Although, that's got less to do with my pregnancy and more to do with everything else."

"So…how *are* things?"

"Complicated," she replied. "I'm a lousy wife and a terrible daughter."

"Well, in the daughter department, I can tell you from experience that sometimes you simply have to do what's best for *you*."

"And in the wife department?"

Ash shrugged. "No idea. I've never been a wife. Nor am I likely to be at this rate. I seem to fit into the *friends-only* category with every man in this town and I don't go anywhere to meet anyone else because I'm too busy working, running the ranch or raising my son."

"And the volunteering at the hospital and with the foster kids you take in at your ranch and the little league that you coach," Kayla reminded her friend. "No wonder you don't have time to date."

"Who said anything about dating," Ash said and grinned. "I'm just talking about plain old no-frills, no-strings sex."

Kayla laughed loudly. She'd missed her friends the past few months. She'd spent so much time avoiding everyone in case they worked out she was in a serious relationship with Liam that she'd forgotten how important Ash and Brooke and Lucy were to her. Which meant she had the lousy-friend option covered as well.

"You're not a no-strings kind of girl," Kayla said. "What about Kieran? He's single now and has all the O'Sullivan looks and charm. Plus, he's a doctor."

Ash smiled. "It's the friends thing. We're buddies, that's all. Anyway, I've got too much going on. I have a new kid arriving in two weeks and this one, according to my lawyer cousin in Phoenix—who rang me three days ago begging me to take them for a few weeks—this one is a real doozy."

"Them?" Kayla said and raised a brow.

"Wayward teenage girl with a truckload of abandonment issues and her hopeless, clueless dad."

Kayla's admiration for her friend tripled. "I don't know how you do it. You're the most switched-on person I know *and* you manage to make it look easy."

"It's a facade," Ash said, grinning. "I'm nowhere near as capable as you think."

"I think you are. I just wish I had an ounce of your gumption."

"You do," Ash assured her. "You're just too considerate to let it show. You've always been too thoughtful for your own good. You always think of everyone else, Kayla. You always put the needs of others before your own. You've always been the good daughter, and you've always done the right thing. That's why your parents have taken this whole situation between you and Liam so hard. They didn't expect it. No one did," she added.

"God, that makes me sound so dull and boring."

"You're beautiful and smart and generous and a wonderful friend. That's not boring...that's *you*."

Kayla almost cried and might have if not for Shirley coming to her office to tell her she had a telephone call. Thinking it was Liam or one of the artists being showcased at the benefit, she excused herself and then Ash left with a quick hug and the promise to see her on Friday to help set up. She was surprised to discover that Gwen O'Sullivan was on the line.

"Mrs. O'Sullivan, what can I—"

"Call me Gwen," her mother-in-law said. "I'd like your help with something."

"Oh...sure," Kayla said a little uncertainly.

"I know that your aunt is in town," Gwen said quietly. "Liam told me you visited her in Oregon. And I believe she is staying with your parents?"

"That's right."

"I would like to meet with her...alone. Oh, I'm not going to scratch her eyes out or anything that dramatic," she said when she caught Kayla's surprised gasp. "But there are some things we need cleared up and I'd like to do it without the entire world watching. I was hoping you could facilitate that without anyone knowing. Including my son."

"Why the secrecy?"

"Pride," Gwen admitted. "I've been made a fool of... my life has been made to look foolish. I don't want to add fuel to that by looking like a woman scorned. I understand your loyalty is to your family...but I would truly appreciate your support with this."

Kayla was dumbfounded. "Oh...of course. I'll see what I can do. But Liam—"

"Will think it's a crazy idea and try to talk me out of it," Gwen said. "I know my son. He'll want to be there, he'll want to stand by and protect me in his way. But I need to do this alone. Please, Kayla, promise me you'll say nothing to him?"

We barely talk these days anyhow...even though we live in the same house.

"I promise. I'll call you and let you know."

Kayla was thinking about the other woman's request long after she hung up the phone. She thought about the way she had left things with Liam that morning and decided to ditch her plans on going to her parents for dinner. Right then it seemed more important for her to go home and talk with her husband. She was about to place a call to Kathleen around three o'clock when her aunt unexpectedly arrived at the museum.

"I thought I would come and see where you work," her aunt said and looked around. "My brother said you were a dedicated and accomplished curator." She nodded approvingly. "I can see that he is right about that."

"Thank you," Kayla said and offered her aunt some tea. "Or would you like a tour of the gallery and museum first?"

Kathleen was quick to take the tour and as she showed her aunt around, Kayla acted as an envoy for Gwen and was startled that her aunt readily agreed to meet with the other woman. She made arrangements for the women to meet at her old apartment the following evening.

"I think it's inevitable," Kathleen said quietly. "We have a lot to discuss," she said and sighed. "So, I imagine things are still pretty tense between your father and your husband?"

"Tense?" Kayla echoed. "You could say that."

Kathleen smiled. "Derek always was a hardhead...even before I fell for J.D. I think the age gap between us made him think of me as a daughter rather than a sister. And since our father died when I was so young, Derek sort of filled the role. But he was always overprotective and tried to run my life, if you know what I mean."

Oh, yeah...she knew. "Dad takes his responsibilities seriously."

Kathleen nodded. "He loves his family. And he's a good man. But he's also very unforgiving and stubborn at times. He blamed J.D. for everything that happened and that was unfair. We *both* fell in love. Sure, J.D. was married...but I knew that. It was as much my doing as J.D.'s. But I could never get Derek to see that. In my brother's eyes, J.D. was the guilty one and I was taken advantage of by an older man." She sighed again. "But it wasn't like that at all. Back then I loved J.D. with all my heart. It didn't matter that he was the one man I *shouldn't* have wanted."

Kayla almost laughed at the familiar sound of her aunt's words.

You could have had any man you wanted. Why him? Why O'Sullivan's son? When you knew what it would do to us.

The pain in her father's voice still haunted her. And she suspected it always would. She swallowed hard and looked at her aunt. "Do you still love him?"

Her aunt took a moment to answer. "I've been torn between loving him and hating him for three decades. Loving that he didn't abandon me and wanted to be a father to our son. And also hating that he didn't abandon me—because that didn't allow me to find love with another man. He's been on the edge of my life for thirty years, but married to another woman. A fine woman who deserved better. And he has tried to be part of Jonah's life. But mostly, that's been a disaster."

"Because Jonah won't accept him as his father?"

"I told my son the truth," she explained. "He's always

known about J.D.'s other family. His father's *real* family, as he likes to put it. Sometimes I think I should have run away and changed my name and started a life on my own. But I was young and scared and shamefully can admit that I welcomed J.D.'s presence in my life in those first few years after my son was born. It made me feel safe, somehow, knowing he was there, even if he did live in another state. But Jonah…" Her words trailed off and she let out a painful, angst-ridden sigh. "My son is filled with so much rage and resentment that sometimes I could weep for how angry he is at his father, just for *being* his father."

Kayla's eyes heated and she blinked her tears away. "Well, maybe being here will help ease some of that anger. I mean, he's got brothers and three little nieces and another niece or nephew on the way," she said and touched her belly. "That's family. And that means something."

"You know what, that means *everything*. And I'm sure my brother will figure that out, too."

"I hope so," Kayla said quietly. "Dad seems to want to hang on to his resentment."

"Because he doesn't want to get hurt," Kathleen said. "And he doesn't want to see you hurt, either. He's spent so many years convincing himself that the O'Sullivans are the bad guys he can't see them as anything else. And certainly not his son-in-law. Do you really love Liam?" Kathleen asked bluntly.

"Yes."

"Then that's all that matters."

"I wish it was," Kayla said with an aching heart. By the time her aunt left it was near closing time, and when she arrived home it was after six, but the house was empty and only Peanuts came to greet her. She fed the cat, then headed upstairs to shower and change her clothes. By eight she was pacing the floorboards, resisting temptation to text Liam and ask when he was coming home. He'd told her he would be home late. She just didn't know how late that was going to be. By eight thirty she was in bed, trying to read. By nine she was staring at the ceiling and waiting to hear Liam's Silverado pull up in driveway. It was after nine thirty when she spotted lights beaming briefly through the window. She waited until she heard the front door open and then slipped out of bed, ignored her robe and slippers and headed downstairs. There was a light on in the kitchen and she followed the glow from the hallway. Liam stood by the window, dressed in jeans, a white polo and runners.

"Hi."

He turned and met her gaze. "I woke you?"

She shook her head. "No. I was awake."

"How was dinner with your folks?"

She shook her head. "I didn't go."

"Why not?"

Her gaze traveled over him. "I thought it was more important that I stay home so we could talk."

His expression was unreadable. "About what?"

"About *us*." She shrugged fractionally. "I... We... You're home late."

"I said I would be."

His quiet tone defied the temper she knew was simmering beneath the surface. The distance between them seemed wider than ever. She'd naively believed that Kathleen's return would be a magic tonic for everything that was wrong with their relationship. But while her parents appeared to be happier and delighted that the other woman was back in their lives, the rift between the two families seemed no closer to being resolved. And their marriage was slam in the middle of all the drama. It didn't help that they'd parted badly that morning—again.

"And you changed your clothes?"

"It was a long day. I used the gym at the hotel and then changed into this. Why?" he queried, one brow cocked at an angle. "Are you suspicious of my movements? Do you think that perhaps your father was right and I've been out screwing around somewhere?"

The silence in the room was suddenly a screeching, chilling sound.

Kayla's hand came to her heart. "Of course not." She took a step closer. "Is that why you're sleeping downstairs... because of something my father said?"

"No," he flipped back. "Because you allowed him to say it in the first place."

Bam. A sucker punch. There was no more skirting around her feelings. Just the accusation that she was a coward, afraid to stand up for herself and do what he clearly considered her responsibility as his wife. "I couldn't say—"

"I would defend you with my dying breath, do you know that?"

Yes...

Kayla took a step closer and grabbed the back of a chair. The pure, undiluted frustration in his expression reached deep down and she took a long, steadying breath. "I'll talk to my father. I'm sure things will be better now that—"

"Better for who?" he said, cutting her off. "Your family? I guess things are working out for your parents now that Kathleen is back, right?"

She nodded. "Of course they're happy. They've missed my aunt terribly and everyone is delighted that she..." Her words trailed off. Of course, *her* family might be celebrating, but Liam's was falling apart quite spectacularly. She felt selfish down to her core. There was not going to be a happy ending for J.D. and Gwen O'Sullivan's marriage. And in that moment, Kayla wondered if her own was going to suffer the same fate. "I'm really sorry that things worked out the way they have for your parents. I know it must be hard on you and Kieran and—"

"Marriages fall apart," he said coolly. "Even those that are believed to be the strongest. I don't blame Kathleen for anything. My mother has made it very clear that she's been unhappy for a long time. And frankly, I'm more concerned about my own marriage, rather than my parents', at the moment."

Kayla stared at him. There it was—Liam O'Sullivan and his absolute truth. No shades of gray...just his black-and-white assertion that their relationship was in trouble.

"I want this to work, Liam... I want us to get through this. For our child's sake."

He went to speak and then stalled. He simply looked at her. Through her. As though he was memorizing every feature, every angle and every expression. Kayla's heart thundered under his intense scrutiny and she matched his gaze, unwavering in her stare.

Finally, he spoke. "You should get some sleep."

She nodded, turned and walked from the room, knowing they'd never been as far apart as they were in that strained, unhappy moment.

Liam had no illusions about his mood. It was bad. And as much as he tried keeping his cool the following day, every so often he would snap. Mostly at Connie, who would shake her head and tell him to take a pill.

He'd left the house before Kayla that morning and hadn't contacted her all day. He checked his watch, saw that it was three o'clock and sent her a brief text message, saying he'd bring dinner home. It wasn't much of an icebreaker, but it would have to do. He waited for a reply, and when one didn't come, pushed the phone aside and immersed himself in work.

Twenty minutes later, Connie popped her head around the office door. She looked a little flustered and he instantly thought there must be some kind of crisis downstairs.

"What's wrong?"

She had a tight smile on her face. "Your brother's here to see you."

Good. He could do with the company. "Kieran? Tell him to come in."

She shook her head. "Not that one," she said, almost whispering. "The other one."

Not Sean, since he was in LA. Liam rounded out his shoulders. *Jonah*. "Send him in."

"Oh… Sure."

Liam frowned. "Everything okay, Connie? Has *he* said something to upset you?"

She shook her head and opened the door wider. "Ah… he's just…he's…no."

"You sure? You look…rattled."

Connie's eyes widened for a second. "Of course I'm not. I'll send him in." Then she swiveled on her heels and disappeared.

A few moments later his newest and youngest brother came through the door. Liam had to admit that they did indeed look alike. There was certainly no doubt that Jonah Rickard was an O'Sullivan.

"Something I can do for you?" Liam asked and pushed his chair back.

His brother walked across the room and dropped into a chair. "Nice hotel you have here."

"The best around."

"J.D. said you were responsible for its success."

Liam almost heard a note of begrudging respect in the other man's voice. "You call him J.D?" he queried. "Why not Dad?"

His brother's eyes narrowed. "Is that any of your business?"

"Probably not," he said and shrugged. "Only if it affects my father. *Our father.*"

Jonah's shoulders twitched. "It's easier. Less confusing."

"For who?"

"Everyone," he replied.

"You hate him that much?" Liam asked bluntly.

"Don't you?" Jonah shot back and sprang from his seat like a caged animal. "He lied to you for thirty years. Aren't you as mad as hell with him?"

"It wouldn't change anything."

Jonah shook his head. "What's wrong with you? How can you sit there so calm and in control? Don't you *feel* anything?"

Liam's gut rolled and he curled his fingers into his palms. The guy certainly had a way of getting under his skin, but he knew getting angry was pointless. Jonah had to fight his own demons his own way. "Just because I'm not punching walls or knocking out teeth doesn't mean I'm happy with my father's behavior. I understand you have issues with him, and rightly so, but he—"

"So, you don't care how he treated you all for years? The contempt? The betrayal?" The rising rage emanating from the younger man was palpable and Liam slowly got to his feet. "You want to know why I don't want anything to do with him. Why I call him *J.D.*? Because I care about my mother."

"Likewise," Liam said quietly. "Which is why fits of temper are counterproductive. *My* mother is divorcing *our* father, did you know that? Making it harder for them both from the sidelines won't change anything. It's the same for your mom... Being angry at our father isn't a way to show you care about her."

Jonah laughed humorlessly. "Maybe you can't understand this, but being an only child is different. When there's only you, and no other siblings to fight with, to confide in, to share what sometimes feels like a goddamned burden of being overloved, you feel responsible. There's no way out of it. No way to stop being the center of their world without hurting them…and that's…unthinkable. When you're an only child, it's as though duty and responsibility are somehow imprinted in your DNA and there's nothing you can do about it."

Liam stilled instantly. Jonah's words were suddenly etched into his brain. *Duty and responsibility.* Didn't he have the same imprint? Hadn't he stepped into his father's shoes without resistance fifteen years ago because he saw it as his job, his familial obligation, to take over the reins and ensure that every member of the family was taken care of?

Duty and responsibility.

Of course.

And then all he could think of was his wife. Kayla and her unrelenting faith in her family. Kayla and her inability to hurt her parents. Kayla and her sweet lips and soft hands.

He'd told her he understood…but it was an understanding on *his* terms.

When he should have given her his complete and unfailing support from the onset. He knew how hard she had struggled with hurting her parents and he'd made all the right noises about understanding her motives, but when it came to the crunch, he'd behaved like an impatient idiot. A demanding idiot. Then he'd moved out of their bed to punish her because she wouldn't bend to his will. No wonder she had pulled away.

He found himself smiling and then grabbed his keys. He looked at Jonah and then walked toward him. The man in front of him was his brother. His kin. His family. Whether he liked it or not.

"Thanks," he said and then slapped Jonah on the shoulder with the same kind of brotherly regard he would show Kieran or Sean. "If you need anything, ask Connie," he said and grinned. "Just try not to upset her. She's got a fearsome temper and is very protective."

He walked out of the office, told Connie he was leaving as he passed her desk and headed downstairs. A few minutes later he was striding through the door of the museum, expecting to find his wife at work. But she wasn't there.

"She left early," Shirley said cheerfully. "I think she said she was going back to her old apartment for something."

Liam thanked the older woman and headed for his vehicle. He considered texting his wife, but changed his mind. They needed to talk face-to-face and her apartment was as good a place as any. Plus, the notion she was at the apartment packing up more of her things pleased him.

He pulled up outside the old Victorian, switched off the ignition and got out. Sure enough, her car was parked in the driveway. But strangely, so was his mother's. He headed inside and took the stairs to her apartment, quickly tapping on the door and was stunned to find his mother and Kathleen Rickard in the midst of an earnest conversation. And no Kayla.

"She's upstairs," Kathleen explained. "Giving us a chance to talk."

Upstairs? With the geek who had the hots for her? Right.

Liam took about three seconds to turn and race up the stairwell. He wrapped his knuckles hard on the door and waited. The door swung back and the geek faced him, looking dishevelled and wary.

"I'm looking for my wife," he said coolly.

The other man stepped aside and Liam immediately

saw Kayla, sitting on the geek's couch, legs curled up, a mug between her hands, looking like she'd done the same thing a thousand times. The very concept that she was in another man's living room, clearly relaxed and in a good mood, curdled his blood with a kind of unholy rage. And despair. And a hurt so intense he felt as though he could barely draw a breath. He stared at her, caught between anguish and anger.

She got to her feet quickly and moved toward the door. "Liam... I...I didn't expect to see you here."

His gaze narrowed. "Clearly."

"We were just—"

"Save the explanation," he said and held up a dismissive hand. "I want you to collect whatever possessions you have left in the apartment and then go home. You won't be coming back here again."

"Liam I—"

"And I don't want you within ten feet of my wife," he said to the other man, now hovering behind them.

Then he turned on his heels and left.

Chapter Eleven

He'd moved out. And into the hotel.

She'd called Liam. Left a message. Sent a text. And got nothing other than a curt reply saying he was at the hotel. No reason. No excuse.

But she knew why. He was angry at the scene at Dane's apartment.

Okay…so it may have looked *bad*, but there was nothing clandestine or questionable about her reason for being there. She'd simply been giving Gwen and Kathleen a chance to speak privately, *and* informing her landlord that she was finally ending her lease and would try to sublet the place. The tea and conversation on the couch was merely a by-product of that. Talking down to Dane was out of line. Moving out was extreme. Ridiculous. If only he'd give her a chance to explain. Stubborn, impossible man!

Kayla had spent her first night alone in the house by the river. She got up at six after spending most of the night tossing in the big bed or staring at the ceiling. Without him in it, the house seemed huge and empty. And now, on Friday morning, she was working on autopilot.

Once she was at work, Kayla spent the morning talking to the caterers and dishing out instructions to the hire company that was providing the tables and chairs for the benefit the following evening. At ten o'clock Ash and Connie stopped by to help set up the tables and by midday she was confident the event would run smoothly and ticked several things off her to-do list. But she was kidding herself. She had one thing on her mind. *Liam*. By one o'clock she'd had enough, and with Shirley managing things, she left the museum and headed down the block to O'Sullivan's. The foyer was busy and she knew several guests had arrived early for the benefit.

She headed upstairs and met Connie in the outer office.

"Liam's not here," Connie said and smiled. "He's talking with the chef, but I can call him if you like?"

"I'll wait," Kayla said and managed a smile. "And don't forget to pick up your dress from Alma's today. When I collected my gown they said you still needed a final fitting."

Connie shrugged. "It'll be fine. Nothing a safety pin won't fix."

Kayla noticed that the other woman seemed distracted as she moved items around on her desk. "Everything okay, Connie?"

She looked up. "Yes…of course."

Kayla wasn't convinced. "If you need to talk…"

Connie looked hesitant, then stopped what she was doing and met her gaze. "Okay…have you ever done something so completely out of character that you can't quite believe it?"

Kayla's brows rose dramatically. "You're asking *me* that?"

The other woman gave out a brittle laugh. "I did something foolish and I can't undo it." She sighed. "But enough about me. So, I guess your secret relationship isn't such a secret anymore?"

"Not exactly," Kayla replied and grinned. "Thank you, by the way, for staying quiet about the whole thing for as long as you did."

Connie shrugged. "I'm not much for gossip. It's been quite an interesting few weeks, though...with everything that's gone on."

"You mean with my aunt and Jonah? Yes, interesting just about covers it."

Connie dropped her gaze back to the table and flicked a few keys on the computer. "Well, I'm sure it will all work out for...everyone. You can wait in Liam's office if you like."

Liam turned up about ten minutes later—enough time for Kayla to stew on the fact that he'd acted like an arrogant, autocratic ass in front of her landlord *and* moved out without giving her a chance to explain. When he walked through the office door she was prepared to give it to him in spades, but one look at him and her anger subsided a little. Because he looked terrible. Exhausted. He was pale and there were dark circles below his eyes. For a moment she wondered if he was coming down with the flu.

He saw her sitting on the chair by the window, but didn't say a word. Instead, he moved around his desk and pulled a bottle of aspirin from the drawer, shaking out a couple of pills and tossing them in his mouth. Then he turned to face her and she saw his bloodshot eyes. Okay, maybe not the flu.

"Are you hungover?"

He winced, as though the sound of her voice made his head hurt. "That's usually what comes from drinking two-thirds of a bottle of whiskey."

"You don't drink."

He raised a brow briefly. "Apparently I do."

"You didn't come home last night. I got your text... I was worried. I thought..."

"You thought what?"

She shrugged. "That you'd moved out."

He winced again and took a shallow breath. "I wasn't in any fit state to drive last night."

"I would have picked you up or—"

"Let's just say I wasn't in any fit state to be *around* last night," he said, cutting her off. "I came back here, met my brothers in the bar and grabbed a bottle of Jack. Drank until I was numb and then I slept right there," he said and pointed to the sofa by the wall.

Kayla took a steadying breath. "Liam. Last night...how it looked... I want you to know I—"

"It looked like you were in another man's apartment and sitting on his couch. And if I acted like a jealous husband, that's because that is exactly what I was last night."

"And today?"

He shrugged lightly. "Today I probably have a little more clarity in my thinking."

Relief worked its way through her. He hadn't moved out. He wasn't angry. "I was giving your mom and Kathleen privacy. Gwen asked if I would arrange a meeting between herself and my aunt...away from the rest of the family."

"Nice of you to let me know."

"She also asked me not to say anything," Kayla explained. "And I didn't like keeping it from you, but she insisted. She was worried you would try and talk her out of it."

"I probably would have," he said. "My mother has been through a lot these last couple of years. Losing Liz nearly broke her. I won't simply stand by and allow her to be hurt again."

"Of course not," Kayla said, her heart lurching forward. Whatever Liam's flaws, his need to protect those he loved was as intrinsic to him as breathing. He was an honorable man and he expected the same in return. "I'm sorry about Dane and how it—"

"How it looked?" he said, cutting her off. "How *you* looked? Relaxed. Happy. You had a life before me, Kayla," he said, clearly frustrated and nursing a headache. "I get that. So did I. We both have a past, we both have friends who we care about and old lovers who might cross our path every now and then and I—"

"Dane was never my lover," she interjected, indignant and fighting the exasperation clamoring through her blood.

"I know that," he said quietly. "And I know it's irrational, but if you'd been sitting in Ash's or Lucy's living room I wouldn't have reacted that way." He shrugged his broad shoulders. "But it *wasn't* Ash or Lucy's living room, was it? And if that sounds like some stupidly macho double standard, well…that's because it is."

As expected, Liam always spoke the absolute truth. He wouldn't color it with lies. Not ever. "We were only talking. I told him I would be subletting the apartment until the lease ran out. That's all." She sighed heavily. "And you would have been welcome to stay. He respects that I'm married and even before that there was nothing between us except friendship. I promise you. But," she added and wagged a finger, "that doesn't mean you have the right to act all stupidly macho and scare the living daylights out of him."

Liam gave a rueful grin and then ran a frustrated hand through his already tousled hair. "I think that seeing you together, looking so relaxed and happy, I just flipped out. Knowing you could talk to him, when we can barely discuss the weather without getting into an argument…it cut deep."

Kayla's heart felt as though it might burst in her chest.

"I'm sorry… I didn't think it through that way. And if it had been the other way around I probably would have reacted the same way."

"You know, I've never considered myself the jealous type," he admitted wearily. "But then…I've never been in love before, so I guess that's clouding my usual good sense."

Kayla's insides rolled over and she rose to her feet. She was about to cross the room and head directly for his arms when the office door opened and his father and Kieran walked across the threshold. J.D. O'Sullivan looked unusually old and tired and Kieran's bloodshot eyes and gray pallor indicated he was in the same state as his brother.

"Women!" J.D. said on a huff, obviously not spotting Kayla. "Damned contrary creatures! You'd think that after thirty-six years of marriage I'd get more than my bags packed on the steps and the door slammed in my face. I can't believe she won't talk to me. She won't even let me take her to that museum thing tomorrow night, when everyone will expect us to arrive together and—" He stopped speaking when he noticed Kayla by the window. "Oh… right…you're here."

"Have either of you heard of the concept of knocking?" Liam asked.

"This used to be *my* office," J.D. said and shrugged. "I figured I was welcome anytime."

Kayla saw the pulse in Liam's cheek throb. They had a half-finished conversation that needed resolution… something she figured they were not going to get while his father and brother were in the room.

She pushed back her shoulders, moved toward her husband and grasped his arm. "I'll see you at home," she said and kissed his cheek. Then she turned toward the other two men. "It's good to see you again, Kieran. Will you be at the benefit tomorrow night?"

"Wouldn't miss it," he replied and grinned. "By the way, welcome to the family."

"Thanks," she said and then faced J.D. "If you're coming tomorrow night, I'd like you to remain civil with my father and with Mrs. O'Sullivan. And remember that the event is about raising money for the hospital, not an opportunity to air grievances or start a squabble...with anyone."

She turned her head, smiled at her husband and then quietly left the room.

"Have I just been put in my place?"

Liam was smiling as he watched his wife leave and then focussed his attention on his father, who was scowling. "Looks like it."

"She's got a lot of sass, that girl."

"Don't I know it," he said and laughed as he glanced at his brother. "You look like hell."

Kieran groaned. "You don't look much better. I don't think I've drunk that much in years."

J.D. puffed out his chest. "That's another thing...did you have to get Jonah trashed last night? Things are bad enough between me and him *and* me and his mother without you two making it worse."

Kieran laughed. "He's got a cast-iron gut and drank us under the table. And I think he made out just fine last night. Last I saw he was wrapped around some blonde in the hall outside his room last night."

Liam ignored his father's scowl. He didn't want to talk about his new brother, his father's battles with Kathleen or his parents' fractured relationship. "Did you two want something?"

"I want you to talk to your mother," J.D. said. "She listens to you."

He considered his father's words and was about to agree,

but something held him back. He looked toward his brother, saw Kieran nodding and then felt an inexplicable kind of relief at the building realization that his parents' marriage wasn't his problem to fix. All his life he'd fixed things, like sorting out squabbles between his younger siblings or taking over the reins of the business. Expansion and growing the O'Sullivan portfolio had been his priority. Even when Liz died, he'd been the glue that kept the family from falling apart. But he couldn't *fix* this.

Absolute truth means absolute control. Over everything.

Kayla's words echoed in his head. She'd accused him of being a control freak. But he couldn't control *this*. It wasn't his to control. He had to stand on the sidelines and allow his parents to work it out for themselves. Without interference. Knowing it would challenge every one of his principles. But he had to do it. He needed to step aside this time.

Instead, he had to work on his own life and marriage.

Before it was too late.

"I have to be somewhere," he said and grabbed his keys and jacket. "You both know the way out." Then he left before they had a chance to reply.

Twenty minutes later he pulled up outside Derek and Marion Rickard's home. His gut was churning, but he knew this was inevitable. Kayla was his wife and the mother of his unborn child. And she needed her parents in her life. They were an important part of who she was. And he had to make it right. Perhaps that meant he would be reasoning with the unreasonable...but he had try.

He got out of the Silverado, turned his phone to mute so he wouldn't be interrupted and headed up the path. It was Kathleen who answered the door and she invited him over the threshold without a word. His mother had met with her the night before and he hoped they had made peace. Kathleen was Jonah's mother, and Jonah, as disagreeable and obnoxious as he seemed, was his blood. Losing his sister had galvanized the importance of family to Liam and he would do what he could to carve out some kind of relationship with his half brother.

"I'd like to see—"

"Derek's in the kitchen," she said and smiled. "Go easy on him, though, will you? He's had a rough couple of days."

He's not the only one.

Liam nodded. "I'll do my best," he said and strode down the hall.

Derek Rickard was inside the pantry, scanning the contents, when Liam entered the room. He took a few steps into the kitchen, crossed his arms and waited.

The older man straightened when he realized he had company and closed the pantry door. "Well, I was wondering how long it would take you."

Liam's shoulders tightened. "Too long, probably. We need to talk."

His father-in-law nodded. "You're right. So…talk. Stand there and tell me that you love my daughter and you'll do anything for her."

Liam sucked in a long breath. "I love your daughter… and I'll do anything for her."

Derek Rickard moved from behind the counter and dropped into a chair. "Love?" His gray brows rose. "You pursued her. You dated her. You married her. You got her pregnant. Knowing," he said with a kind of anguished emphasis, "that it would create a problem between her and her family…do you actually call that *love*?"

He considered the older man's logic. To Derek Rickard, it seemed cut-and-dried. But it wasn't. Liam walked around the table and grasped the back of a chair. "You're right… I pursued her. I pursued her for months before she agreed to go out with me. I pursued Kayla because the night she crashed into my car in the parking lot at the hotel, I got out of my vehicle and took one look at her and felt as though I'd been struck by lightning. I couldn't breathe. I couldn't think. I could barely string two words together. Have you ever felt that? Did you have that feeling when you first met your wife? If so, did you ignore it? Did you walk away? *Could* you have walked away?" His knuckles were white around the chair. "Well, I couldn't. Maybe that sounds foolish...but it's the truth."

Derek looked at him, long and hard. His hands were on the table, linked together. Finally, he spoke. "Yes, actually, I have felt that. When I first met Marion, I thought she was the most beautiful girl I have ever seen and I couldn't wait to see her again. I knew, the moment I met her, that she was all I wanted. She still is."

Liam nodded. "Then you understand. And don't tell me it's different," Liam said and waved a hand when the older man went to protest. "It's no different. Look, I get that you dislike my family and have a problem with everything my father did. Hell, *I've* got a problem with it. However, he's still my father and I have to forgive him for making a monumental mistake that has now broken my family in two. So, if you want to hate me," he said evenly, "then hate *me*. Give it all you've got because I can take it. But what I can't take is my wife's tears and unhappiness because the father she has adored and looked up to all her life is acting like he despises her."

Derek looked as if he wanted to get to his feet and go a few rounds, but to his credit, the older man remained seated. "Do you think I enjoy seeing my daughter unhappy?"

"Not at all," Liam shot back. "But she *is* unhappy and some of that is because of you. Not all of it," he amended.

"I have my own part in this. But right now she needs your support, not your disapproval."

"She's had my support and love since the day she was born."

"Until the moment she did something you didn't approve of," Liam said, pushing down his rising anger. "All I know is this, we both love her…but if you don't learn to at least accept our marriage, at some point one of us is going to lose her. And whichever way that turns out, Kayla is going to be in the middle of a whole lot of heartbreak." Liam took a heavy breath. "As her husband, I can't allow that. And as her father, you shouldn't allow that, either."

Then Liam turned and strode from the room, leaving the other man staring after him.

By the time he got home it was after four o'clock. Kayla's car was parked in the driveway and he was so pleased she was home he rushed from his vehicle and took the steps two at a time.

He found her asleep on the sofa, her legs curled up, and her face resting serenely on her hands. Liam grabbed a cotton throw from the back of the sofa and draped it over her shoulders and then headed upstairs to shower and shave. When he returned downstairs twenty minutes later, dressed in jeans and a black T-shirt, she was still asleep. He dropped into the chair by the window, rested his elbows on the leather arms and linked his fingers together. She looked insanely beautiful as she slept. And peaceful. Without a worry. His gaze traveled down, over her slender neck and throat, and farther to her still-flat belly. Knowing their child was sheltered and growing inside her filled him with a kind of joy he hadn't known he could feel, and a deep-rooted need to keep them protected and safe.

All his life he'd sought to do the right thing…much like Kayla had. He'd been raised to be responsible and to take those responsibilities seriously. To always think of others, but at the same time, expect the best from those around him. In his personal life, he'd dated casually, never getting too close because he didn't want to lead any woman into thinking he was ready to settle down when he wasn't. At work, he was fair, but demanding. His staff, he knew, respected him, but he suspected they also feared him a little. His work ethic, his strict moral code and unflappable belief in the truth above anything else had made him what he was—generous in nature, but also impatient and arrogant. So, when Kayla had asked for time to tell her parents about their relationship, he'd mistaken that as a sign of her reticence and lack of commitment in their relationship. In *him. In them.*

And it had hurt. His heart *and* his pride. He should have had more patience, helped her through the reluctance she was feeling rather than make demands and call her a coward.

His gaze moved back to her face and he saw that her eyes were open.

"You're awake."

"You're staring."

"You're beautiful," he said and smiled. "And I can't help myself. Anyway, you looked as though you needed to rest."

"I did," she replied, unmoving. "I got home an hour ago and flaked out. Growing this baby inside me has made me realize how much I need to rest."

"It's been a long week," he said quietly and nodded, meeting her steady gaze. "I spoke with your father this afternoon."

Her eyes widened immediately. "You did?"

"I went to see him. To talk. I got the feeling he'd almost been expecting me at some point."

"And how did that go?"

"He listened to what I had to say. The rest is up to him."
He edged forward a little. "I get it, you know…how it is
for you. How hard it has been to go against your parents'
expectations…probably for the first time in your life. The
truth is, we both come from close families. But I had three
siblings and growing up we all kind of scrambled for whatever attention we could get, in between one another. And
even though I stepped into my father's shoes and took over
the business, I'm sure that if I'd decided to bail on the business and Cedar River like Kieran and Sean did, my father
would have blustered his way through his disappointment.
He would have sold the hotel and found something else
to spend his money on." He took a long breath and kept
their gaze linked. "But for you, there was only *you*. And
I understand now that it's a different kind of family obligation. A different kind of duty that you feel. That there's
only you and them."

She sat up slowly, crossing her legs. "Why the change
of thinking?"

"My brother."

"Kieran?"

Liam shook his head. "Jonah. He said it was different
for him. He said that being raised as an only child created
a different kind of dynamic. It made me think of you and
then it made sense."

A small smile curved her lovely mouth. "You said he
was your brother?"

Liam shrugged. "Can't change DNA. And I'm going to
try and build some kind of relationship with him…as long
as he meets me partway."

"I'm glad," she said softly. "I think he needs you, even
though he probably doesn't know it yet. And it might help
him to stop being so angry at your dad."

"Maybe," he said and shifted in his seat. "But frankly,

I'm tired of worrying about everyone else's relationships. The only one I'm concerned about right now is this one… you and me."

Her brown eyes shimmered and her smile widened. "Then what are you doing way over there?"

It was all the invitation he needed. He got up and joined her on the sofa, taking her hands in his own. She pressed forward, but Liam pulled back a fraction. "Kayla…let me get this out, let me finish this, and once we're done, then I'd like to spend the next few hours making love to you." He raised her hand to his mouth and kissed her knuckles. "I know I've been impatient and angry and sometimes down-right unbearable during the last few months. Particularly since Vegas. It's no secret that I'm used to getting my own way," he admitted ruefully, holding her hands within his. "When I want something, I usually get it."

"Like me?"

He shrugged. "You knocked me on my ass that day in the parking lot, do you know that? I told your dad today that it was like being struck by lightning. And it was. But my attraction to you made me bullheaded and determined to get you and I didn't really care about the consequences. Even though I knew what they would be."

"That my parents would never accept it?"

He nodded. "And maybe they never will. We have to consider that possibility. And you have to decide if you can handle that. I'll be here, every step of the way with you, but we'll do this at your pace. The whole family knows the truth about Kathleen and Jonah and soon that news will be common knowledge in town…especially now my mother has decided she wants to end her marriage. Which truly sucks," he said and sighed. "But there's nothing I can do about it. Nothing I can say. All I can do is be here for you. For us."

"And my parents?"

"We'll find a way to make it work," he assured her. "But we can only live our life as authentically as possible and hope he can learn to forgive my father or, at least, forgive *me* for falling in love with you."

Her eyes glistened. "I know I shouldn't care," she admitted. "I know I should stand up to my overprotective parents and not care that I might not see them, or talk to them, or that they might miss out on being grandparents to our baby. And I should say to hell with everyone and everything other than you and me and tell the world how I feel about you."

Liam pressed two fingers to her lips. "As long as we tell each other, the rest doesn't really matter. And don't be angry at your parents for loving you and being overprotective. If we have a daughter, I'm pretty sure I'm going to be the most overprotective father on the planet."

Kayla smiled beneath his fingertips and he dropped his hand. She grabbed it and held it firm against her belly. "You're going to be an incredible father. And now," she said and inched closer, "didn't you say something about what you wanted to do for the next few hours?"

Liam chuckled. "I did. Did you have something in mind?"

"We could head down to the boathouse?"

He curved an arm around her waist and eased her close. "We could. Or we stay right here?"

They stayed on the sofa, stripping clothes off.

And they made love to one another, slowly, tenderly. Each kiss lingering longer than the last. Each touch more gentle than the one before. Every slide of skin against skin more intense than any had ever been between them in the past. And finally, when she lay beneath him, her arms and body welcoming him to move inside her, her eyes shining bright with pleasure and emotion she couldn't hide, Liam was completely and totally lost in all that she was.

Her beauty. Her goodness. Her tenderness. *Her love*. He claimed her. She claimed him. She *owned* him, body and soul. In that moment there was no one else in the world and he could only say what was in his heart.

"I love you, Kayla."

Chapter Twelve

When Kayla woke she was alone. It was Saturday morning and the clock read eight fifteen. The sheets beside her were still warm and she sighed a lovely and contented sigh when she remembered how much loving they'd done during the night. First on the sofa, and then later when Liam carried her upstairs.

She swung her legs off the bed, grabbed her robe, slid her arms into it and tied the belt. She wandered to the window and stared out, immediately spotting Liam down by the jetty. He was looking out across the water and as she watched him, a wave of intense love washed over her.

With everything that had happened between them in the past couple of weeks, one thing remained strong…the love between them was as it had been from the beginning. She felt it as though it was a tender cloak wrapped around her shoulders and giving her the strength to get through anything.

And she would.

She'd spent her life whole trying to please the people she loved...from dance class, to the calculus club in high school. From getting into a great college and finishing her degree to landing a job back in Cedar River...because it was what her parents wanted. Because it validated the unending love they had given her throughout her life. Pleasing them made her feel good about who she was. It justified their belief in her. It made her the *perfect daughter.*

And robbed her of the ability to make her own decisions and live by them.

But then, she thought as she touched her belly and looked toward the jetty, things had spectacularly imploded. She'd fallen for the one man her parents disapproved of most. She'd dated him, fallen in love with him, married him and then made a baby with him...in secret.

And that secrecy had devalued every single moment they had shared together.

Shame, as hot as hellfire, started up her ankles and licked her calves and thighs, working its way up her abdomen, and then landed squarely in the center of her chest.

I'm such a coward.

She'd never considered herself cowardly. *Good daughters* weren't cowards. They were kind and considerate and loving and...*good.* A good daughter made her parents proud. A good daughter *always* put others first. The years of programming, the years of being told she was their miracle child, their whole world, their *everything*...that love had somehow become a *burden.* An albatross. A weight of responsibility so heavy she hadn't been able to see anything else other than her almost desperate need to please them.

And then she had crashed into Liam's car and her whole belief system had derailed.

She looked toward the jetty and wondered what he was

thinking in that moment. Liam had been open about his feelings from the beginning. He hadn't shied away from their attraction because he'd believed it was stronger than any old family squabbles. And he was right. She'd simply been too blinded by duty and obligation to realize the truth.

But no more.

If their marriage was to survive, she needed to take hold of her gumption and make things right. For Liam. For herself. For the baby soon to come into the world.

Kayla grabbed her cell phone and quickly made a few calls. By the time she was done she felt better, stronger, and resilient and empowered. The woman she had always believed herself to be.

Once she dressed, she headed downstairs and found Liam coming through the back door. He looked so handsome in jeans and a brown checked shirt that her heart flipped over.

"We should get a dog," he said and smiled.

"Good morning to you, too," she said, laughing. "A dog? That's quite a commitment."

"It goes hand in hand with the whole marriage and babies and a cat thing, don't you think?"

Kayla wrinkled her nose. "I'm not sure Peanuts will agree. But, if that's what you want."

He shrugged and then looked more serious. "I'd like the peace of mind, you know, of having someone standing on point when I'm not here. When I was down on the jetty just now I realized how isolated this place actually is. It would make me feel better if we had a hound sitting on the porch, watching over things."

"So, we're talking a big dog? Like the ones Ash has?" Kayla asked, thinking of her friend's pair of Ridgebacks.

"Exactly. We could go to the shelter in Deadwood next week and choose one."

For the next hour they were at the kitchen table, looking on his laptop at animal shelters in the county, in between eating eggs and toasted sourdough. It seemed achingly normal. Without tension. Without anything interfering. Until Liam's cell rang.

"I have to go," he said, ending the call and then kissing her forehead. "The sous chef had an accident and I have to meet Abby at the restaurant. Looks like he got knocked over in the parking area and broke his leg. I don't know how long I'll be. I have to fill out a report on the accident and head over to the hospital, but I'll call you later."

She nodded. "I'm heading out soon. I have a few errands to run and then I'll be at the museum most of the afternoon preparing for the benefit. I'll probably get dressed there."

He nodded, promised to call as soon as he was done with the emergency and then left quickly. Kayla cleaned up, missing him as she lingered in the house for an hour and then headed to her parents' home at midday.

There were several cars parked by the curb and she recognized most of them.

The door was open and she could hear voices. Her parents, J.D. and Gwen O'Sullivan, Kathleen and Jonah, and her grandmother were all in the living room, in various stages of conversation. J.D. and Gwen were standing by her grandmother. Her parents were huddled in one corner, with her dad giving death stares to J.D, while Kathleen was pouring coffee on a tray at the sideboard and Jonah stood alone by the fireplace, looking bored and as though he wanted to be somewhere else.

Kayla stood by the door and watched. These people were her family. By either blood or marriage, they were now her child's family, too, and she wanted them in her baby's life.

But only on her terms.

She cleared her throat and seven sets of eyes immediately zoomed to her direction.

"Kayla," her father said. "What's the meaning of this? Is this all your doing? Why have you asked everyone to—"

"Yes," she said and took a deep breath. "It's my doing, Dad. I asked everyone to come here today."

"Asked?" J.D. said and made a scoffing sound. "Demanded, you mean. And where's my son? He should be—"

"He's at the hotel," she explained. "I wanted to talk to you all...alone."

"Kayla, this is—"

"Please, Dad," she said and raised a hand. "I need to speak to all of you, all together, so no one misinterprets what I have to say."

The silence was suddenly deafening, but she wasn't deterred. If she backed down, it would never be said, never be resolved. And that was unthinkable. There was too much at stake for her to back out now.

"I know there's a lot of anger and resentment in this room," she said and looked at everyone in turn. "I know some of it has been there for a long time. And like any feeling that's had a lot of years invested in it, letting go is difficult. Sometimes impossible. Friendships have been lost," she said, looking at her father and J.D. "And maybe they'll never be what they were. But I'd like to think we can all learn to get along."

"Consider it water under the bridge, you mean?" Gwen O'Sullivan suggested.

Kayla nodded. "Exactly."

"Easier for some," her father said and scowled.

"I get it, Dad," she said and sighed. "I get that you're angry and probably won't ever get past this...but that's okay. I can live with that. The thing is, can you?" Before he could reply, she went on. "Six months ago I did something no one expected…including myself. I fell in love… I fell in love with a man I was always told to stay away from. A man I was told was cold and unfeeling and didn't care about anything but wealth and power. But you couldn't be more wrong," she said and met her father's gaze. "Liam is the most generous person I have ever known. He's kind and honest and incredibly good. Of course, he can also be arrogant and stubborn and likes things done his own way… but he has this amazing integrity that is unflappable." She looked toward Liam's parents and sighed. "You know this about him already. You know that he would never lie, never cheat, never do anything he'd consider dishonorable."

Gwen's eyes shimmered and she nodded. "That's very true."

Kayla swallowed the lump in her throat and looked at her father again. "You see, Dad, he's really not that much different from you. Liam is the most honorable person I have ever known. Like you. So, it's not surprising that I fell for him as I did. And despite how badly I have behaved toward him these past few months…how much I have hurt him over and over and how I've refused to acknowledge our relationship, and how I've been afraid to tell my family and my friends that I am undeniably and completely in love with this man, he still believes in me. He still wants me. He still *loves* me. And that just beats all," she said and smiled, blinking at the tears in her eyes. "Don't you think? So, Mom, Dad…don't ask me to choose. Don't ask me to give him up or to give up on our marriage…because I won't. Not ever. But I don't want to give up on you, either."

There was more silence, stretching out like frayed elastic. Kayla was about to turn and leave when her grandmother got up from her chair, walked across the room and stood at her side.

Grams grabbed her hand and squeezed it tightly and

Kayla felt the old woman's support through to her bones. She had an ally and it gave her more strength than she'd imagined.

Then Grams spoke. "Right…so now, you're all on notice. You heard my granddaughter…she loves him. He loves her. And I've had about enough of all this squabbling." She looked toward Kathleen. "I'm glad my daughter had the sense to come home and sort this out and I'm glad I finally got to meet my grandson," she said and glanced in Jonah's direction. "The rest of you need to learn to get along. There's a baby coming. A baby that you will share as a grandchild. So get over your bickering and grow up."

Kayla kissed her grandmother's cheek. "Thanks, Grams. You're the best."

"Life is too short to hold grudges," Grams said, grinning, and then looked toward her son. "You might want to think about that, Derek. I lost a child for thirty years," she said and glanced at Kathleen and then toward J.D. and Gwen. "And when their daughter, Liz, died, they lost one forever. I hope you never know that feeling, Derek. But if you keep up this anger, if you keep pushing and can't learn to forgive, you just might."

They were defining words in a defining moment.

Then there were tears and hugs and when her father walked across the room and took Kayla in his arms, tears on his cheeks, she held on to him, knowing everything would somehow work out. She loved her parents, but she loved Liam, too.

Now, all she had to do was tell him.

And the world.

"Is there someone we should call?"

Liam was standing in the hospital corridor, talking with Lucy and Abby about the sous chef, who was now sporting a broken leg and two cracked ribs courtesy of an unlicensed driver losing control of his car in the parking area outside the hotel.

"Connie's checked his employee details and called his next of kin," he said and nodded. "His sister is on her way from Rapid City. Thanks for taking care of him so quickly."

"That's my job," Lucy said. "I'll come back and check on him later."

Once she left, he assisted Abby with the more formal details around the accident and then headed back to the hotel around three. He called Kayla and told her he'd shower and dress at the hotel and would meet her later at the museum. Staff accidents required immediate attention and he spent most of the afternoon filling out the necessary incident and insurance forms. The hotel was busy and it was after five thirty by the time he was ready to leave for the benefit. Connie was at her desk, dressed up in a red gown instead of her usual black skirt and hotel jacket. She was distracted and he was about to ask her what was wrong when Derek Rickard appeared in the entrance to the outer office. Connie immediately excused herself, grabbing her bag before she headed off and said she'd see him at the museum.

Liam waited for the other man to speak. And didn't have to wait long.

"This is the thing…despite everything…my daughter is the most important person in the world to me."

"And to me," Liam said quietly.

He nodded. "And I only want her to be happy."

"That's good to hear."

Derek let out a weary sigh. "What your father did was wrong. But…that was him and it was a long time ago. So, I know it might not seem like it…but I have no beef with you, son."

Liam stilled instantly. "You don't?"

The other man shrugged. "Earlier today my daughter told me that you were the most honorable man she has ever known. And it occurred to me that I have no reason to doubt her. You know, I never imagined anyone would come along who would cherish her more than I do...but it seems that I was wrong. So, even though it doesn't make a difference. Even though it doesn't matter one iota what I think...you have my blessing."

Liam's chest tightened. He knew he shouldn't care. But he did. Because he knew what it would mean to Kayla. "Thank you."

Derek sighed unevenly. "My daughter loves you very much. She made that abundantly clear to all of us today."

Liam frowned. "All of who?"

The other man spent a good two minutes informing him of the O'Sullivan invasion into his home earlier that day and Kayla's impassioned speech. Love, pure and simple, washed over him like a wave. And gratitude. Because she'd stood up for him. For them. For their marriage. At last. And he couldn't have loved her more than he did in that moment.

"Well, isn't there a fancy party we all have to go to?" Derek asked.

He nodded. "You do know my father will be there?"

"I know." The other man half smiled. "But between his wife and my sister and that moody son of his, I reckon he's got bigger problems than me."

Liam laughed. "Yeah, I think you're right."

And if anyone had told him a couple of weeks ago that he'd be walking through the doors of the museum on the evening of the benefit beside Derek Rickard, he wouldn't have believed a word of it. Nonetheless, Liam arrived just after six o'clock and most of the guests were already in attendance. Tables were set up along one wall, and wait staff were busy moving around the crowd, offering trays of canapés and drinks. The place was humming with a kind of animated energy and he stopped every few strides to greet people he knew and who recognized him. There was a small stage off to one side and an instrumental trio were playing some kind of classical tune.

When he spotted Connie talking to Lucy Monero and her fiancé, Brant Parker, he quickly headed for them.

"Have you seen Kayla?" he asked, scanning the crowd.

"Last I saw she was with Brooke and Tyler at the back of the gallery," Connie replied.

He excused himself and wove a path through the crowd. He saw Kieran and his mother and acknowledged them as he walked toward the gallery. And then he saw her. Radiant in a long, dark blue dress that draped around her waist and was secured at her neck in a halter style. She'd never looked more beautiful.

She must have sensed his presence, because her head turned and she met his gaze, smiling. And there it was. *The lightning.* That intense connection and longing he had for her...and only her. It struck him way down low and then cascaded through his body like a bonfire. He met her halfway across the room, suddenly oblivious to everything and everyone else. He knew they were being watched. Cedar River was a small town and their relationship would be news on the small-town grapevine. But he ignored the stares. He ignored everything except his lovely wife making her way toward him.

"You look so beautiful," he said and grasped her right hand when she reached him.

"You look pretty good yourself," she said and moved closer. "Have you come to help me schmooze and sell some of this amazing artwork for charity?"

"Absolutely. The place looks incredible. And the turn-out is good. Better than we hoped."

"Three pieces of art have already sold," she said, clearly delighted. "And there have been bids on four others. At this rate we'll reach our goal well before the end of the evening. I have to give a speech soon...you know, thanks to the artists who donated their work and to the people who've helped this night come together."

"I'm really proud of you. This event is all your doing."

"Not all," she corrected. "I couldn't have done it without your support and guidance. So, thank you. By the way, your parents are here," she said and her mouth flattened a little. "Not together, I might add. Your mom arrived with Kieran and your dad arrived alone. But at least they're *here*."

"As are yours. But I don't think we're in for any fireworks tonight," he said and grinned. "I'm sure everyone will be on their best behavior. Even Jonah."

She laughed softly. "I think I saw him hanging around the door looking for his first chance to escape."

"I'm sure he'll do his best to have a terrible time," Liam said and rubbed her fingers. "But you never know, he might surprise us. Speaking of surprises," he said and led her off to the side to a little alcove so they could speak privately. "Your father came to see me this afternoon. I think we've come to an understanding."

She nodded, as though it was no surprise at all. "I'm glad. I hope he can find some place of peace where *your* father is concerned. Once the baby comes, there'll be a christening and then birthdays... I want to share that with my family. With *our* families."

"We will," he promised and touched her stomach discreetly. "How's our little champ doing?"

"She's good."

"She?"

Kayla smiled. "Just a feeling."

"I hope you're right," he said softly, grabbed her hand

and brought it to his mouth. "I like the idea of my daughter having me wrapped around her finger, just like her mom." Something glittered on her hand and he turned her palm over. The platinum-and-diamond band he'd slipped onto her finger that night in Vegas over a month ago was securely in its place. "You're wearing your ring?"

She nodded. "For good. Forever. I love you, Liam. More than that, I need you. Always. And I'm sorry it's taken me so long to say the words to you. I'd tell the world if I could."

Like stars aligning, Liam experienced a strange and almost surreal sense of peace that started deep down in his chest and then worked its way across his skin and through every molecule he possessed.

"You're saying them to me," he said and touched her cheek. "And that's all that matters. So, go give your speech and when you're done we'll do that schmoozing you wanted."

She smiled and stepped away and he watched her walk through the crowd, her golden hair shimmering beneath the lights. He was about to seek out his father when both his brothers sidled up beside him. Kieran had a beer in one hand and Liam raised a curious brow.

"Hair of the dog," Kieran said and grinned. "You should try it."

Liam grimaced. "I'll pass."

Jonah made a scoffing sound. "You two girls can't hold your liquor."

"Has your blonde from last night given you the slip?" Kieran asked and took a drink.

Technically the youngest O'Sullivan—since he was born three days after Sean—shrugged one shoulder. "Two nights in a row looks too much like a relationship."

"You sentimental fool," Kieran teased.

Liam laughed. Maybe having another brother wasn't so

bad, after all. Jonah was even more uptight than he was. It would be a nice change *not* being considered the most disagreeable O'Sullivan around.

"You look happy," Kieran said and jabbed him in the ribs with an elbow.

"I am," he admitted.

"I almost envy you," his brother said and drank some more beer. "Incidentally, I heard that Kayla wiped the floor with everyone today. Mom said it was something else. It must be nice knowing the woman you love has your back."

Liam looked at Kieran and nodded. "It is."

"Yep. I definitely envy you."

"Now who's being sentimental?" Jonah said just as the music stopped playing.

Liam's attention was quickly drawn to the stage. Kayla stepped onto the small podium and began to speak, her lovely voice filtering throughout the room. And then he felt and heard nothing but her.

Kayla took a deep breath and adjusted the microphone. She'd practiced her thank-you speech a dozen times in her head and the words began to roll off her tongue.

"Thank you so much for coming tonight. My name is Kayla R—" She stopped, meeting Liam's loving gaze across the room and changing her mind midsentence. "My name is Kayla O'Sullivan, and I am the curator of the Cedar River Museum and Art Gallery."

She heard a few gasps, saw a few heads turn in Liam's direction. And also saw him smiling just a little. So, she went on, thanking the artists, the local dignitaries attending, the hospital volunteers, Shirley and Ash and the caterers and anyone else who'd helped pull the event together. When she was almost done, she paused and took a breath. She could see close to one hundred pairs of eyes directed toward her, waiting for her next words. She spotted her parents and saw her dad smile reassuringly.

With her gaze fixed back to Liam, she continued, "And lastly, I'd like to thank my husband, Liam, who has generously funded this evening's event. The O'Sullivan family has a long history of charitable work in our town and I'm very proud to now be a part of that legacy. So, thank you, Liam… I love you more than words can say." She saw his stunned expression, took a breath and smiled. "And thank you to everyone for coming tonight and making the event such a success. Please, enjoy the rest of the evening."

There was a short applause and she quickly handed the microphone back to the musicians and stepped off the stage. She watched as Liam said something to his brothers and then headed directly for her. By the time he reached her Kayla's knees were shaking and her heart was full of love for him.

"So, not exactly the world," he said and grasped her hand, linking their fingers intimately. "But close enough."

She smiled. "I think I've shocked a few people already today."

"Yes," he said and drew her close. "I heard about your family meeting today."

Kayla shrugged and moved into his embrace. "I was staking a claim on what was mine."

"And what's that?" he teased.

"You," she replied. "Us."

"I like the sound of that. Do you know what else I would like?" he said, smiling.

"What?"

His arms tightened around her. "To marry you again," he said, stunning her. "In a chapel in this town with our family and friends around us."

Kayla's heart rolled over. "I'd like that very much."

"So, would you have any objections if I kissed you right about now, Mrs. O'Sullivan?"

"Not one."

His mouth met hers in a sweetly passionate kiss that made her swoon and then smile when she heard a few whoops and cheers around them. It was the happiest moment of her life. And she was happier still, knowing there was more to come. Her life with Liam. Their baby. Their family.

Which was everything.

Epilogue

"So, I have to ask," Liam's brother Sean said as he adjusted his tie for about the third time in as many minutes. "Why are you doing this if you're already hitched?"

Liam glanced at Sean and grinned. "Because I want to marry the woman I love in front of our friends and family. Because I want to see her in a white dress. Because I want my brothers standing at my side for the most important moment in my life. Take your pick," he said and tapped his younger brother on the shoulder.

Sean had arrived in Cedar River less than six hours ago, Kieran the day before. And Jonah two days earlier. He was incredibly grateful that they'd all made the effort to be part of his wedding.He looked at each of his brothers. All three, wearing dark suits with a flower in the lapel, waited for him to make a move and head through the door and into the chapel.

"Thanks for being here," he said. "It means a lot to me."

They all nodded. Even Jonah, who Liam suspected had agreed to be a groomsman despite his continued resistance to the idea he was an O'Sullivan.

"Wouldn't miss it," Kieran said and grinned. "Besides, every time I come home I remember how much I like this town."

Sean groaned. "I knew it, you're gonna move back here, right?"

Kieran shrugged. "Maybe," he said casually. "If I can get on staff at the hospital."

"What about you?" Sean asked, looking at Jonah. "You got any plans to ditch Portland and settle in Cedar River?"

"Not one," Jonah replied. "Although, now that my mother has decided she wants to spend more time here, no doubt I'll be commuting when I want to see her."

Liam looked at the three men. All different. But all bound together by blood. Which felt even more important to him now that he had Kayla and a baby on the way. Now he understood why his father had fought so fiercely to keep Jonah in his life. And why he still did, even though his youngest brother rarely gave J.D. the time of day. *Family.* The only thing in life that truly mattered.

"Okay," he said with a smile and took a deep breath. "Let's do this. I want to go and marry my wife."

Then he turned on his heels and left the room with his brothers right behind him.

As the car pulled up outside the chapel, Kayla experienced another flutter of nerves in her belly. Silly, she supposed, since she and Liam were already married. But, somehow, this truly felt like her wedding day. Maybe it was the beautiful lace dress, or the flowers, or the fact that she was sitting in the back of a limo with her father...whatever the reason, she was brimming with happiness. And a few pre-wedding jitters.

"Everything okay, love?"

She met her father's gaze and smiled. "Fine, Dad. I just can't quite believe I'm here."

Derek's gaze softened. "He's a lucky man."

Kayla smiled. "I'm the lucky one. Liam is the kindest and most amazing person I have ever known and I feel so incredibly blessed to have him in my life. And thank you," she said and gently squeezed her father's arm, "for giving him a chance. I know how difficult it was for you to accept this...to accept us."

Derek shrugged, his eyes glistening a little. "He loves you...that's all I could ask for."

"He does," she said and smiled again. "He really does."

As they stepped from the car, Lucy, Ash and Brooke were quickly by her side, straightening her veil and fluffing her small bouquet of tiny white roses. Kayla ran a hand down the lace gown, felt her small baby bump and sighed happily.

"You ready?" Ash asked, hugging her.

"Absolutely."

Kayla took her father's arm and followed the bridesmaids up the steps and into the chapel. She heard music, saw people rise as Ash, Lucy and Brooke headed down the aisle and waited with her father until it was her turn to follow. She spotted her grandmother and her aunt in the front row and her mother at the end of the aisle, and Liam's parents on the other side.

And then she saw Liam standing by the altar and everything else faded around her. He looked so handsome in his dark suit, and when their gaze met she saw love and longing and her heart brimmed over. When she reached the altar, Liam held out his hand and as her father released her, Kayla moved toward the man she loved, entwining her fingers with his.

"Hello, beautiful," he said, his voice the only sound she could hear.

She smiled and moved closer. "You're here."

His blue eyes glittered brilliantly and he laid a gentle hand against her belly as they turned toward the preacher. "We're here," he said softly.

In that moment, she knew that nothing and no one would ever come between them. They had each other—body, heart and soul. And for always.

* * * * *

Look for Ash's story,
the next installment of
THE CEDAR RIVER COWBOYS
Helen Lacey's new series,
on sale August 2017.

And catch up with Kayla and Liam's friends and family
by reading the previous books in
THE CEDAR RIVER COWBOYS *series*
for Mills & Boon Cherish:

THREE REASONS TO WED
LUCY & THE LIEUTENANT
And
THE COWGIRL'S FOREVER FAMILY

Available wherever Mills & Boon books and ebooks are sold.

MILLS & BOON®

Cherish™

EXPERIENCE THE ULTIMATE RUSH OF FALLING IN LOVE

A sneak peek at next month's titles...

In stores from 6th April 2017:

- **His Shy Cinderella** – Kate Hardy *and* **Fortune's Surprise Engagement** – Nancy Robards Thompson
- **Conveniently Wed to the Greek** – Kandy Shepherd *and* **The Lawman's Convenient Bride** – Christine Rimmer

In stores from 4th May 2017:

- **Falling for the Rebel Princess** – Ellie Darkins *and* **The Last Single Garrett** – Brenda Harlen
- **Claimed by the Wealthy Magnate** – Nina Milne *and* **Her Kind of Doctor** – Stella Bagwell

---

Just can't wait?
Buy our books online before they hit the shops!
www.millsandboon.co.uk

Also available as eBooks.

0417/23

MILLS & BOON®

EXCLUSIVE EXTRACT

When Greek tycoon Alex Mikhalis
discovers Adele Hudson is pregnant
he abandons his plans to get even and
suggests a very intimate solution:
becoming his convenient wife!

Read on for a sneak preview of
CONVENIENTLY WED TO THE GREEK

'What?' The word exploded from her.

'You can't possibly be serious.'

Alex looked down into her face. Even in the slanted
light from the taverna she could see the intensity in his
black eyes. 'I'm very serious. I think we should get
married.'

Dell had never known what it felt to have her head
spin. She felt it now. Alex had to take hold of her elbow
to steady her. 'I can't believe I'm hearing this,' she said.
'You said you'd never get married. I'm not pregnant to
you. In fact you see my pregnancy as a barrier to kissing
me, let alone marrying me. Have you been drinking too
much ouzo?'

'Not a drop,' he said. 'It's my father's dying wish that
I get married. He's been a good father. I haven't been a
good son. Fulfilling that wish is important to me. If I
have to get married, it makes sense that I marry you.'

'It doesn't make a scrap of sense to me,' she said.

'You don't get married to someone to please someone else, even if it is your father.'

Alex frowned. 'You've misunderstood me. I'm not talking about a real marriage.'

This was getting more and more surreal. 'Not a real marriage? You mean a marriage of convenience?'

'Yes. Like people do to be able to get residence in a country. In this case it would be marriage to make my father happy. He wants the peace of mind of seeing me settled.'

'You feel you owe your father?'

'I owe him so much it could never be calculated or repaid. This isn't about owing my father, it's about loving him. I love my father, Dell.'

But you'll never love me, she cried in her heart. How could he talk about marrying someone—anyone— without a word about love?

Don't miss
CONVENIENTLY WED TO THE GREEK
by Kandy Shepherd

Available May 2017
www.millsandboon.co.uk